ME &
MR J

RACHEL McINTYRE

ME &
MR J

First published in Great Britain in 2015
by Electric Monkey – an imprint of Egmont UK Limited
The Yellow Building, 1 Nicholas Road, London W11 4AN

Text copyright © 2015 Rachel McIntyre
The moral rights of the author have been asserted

ISBN 978 1 4052 7344 2

1 3 5 7 9 10 8 6 4 2

58093/1

www.egmont.co.uk

A CIP catalogue record for this title is available from the British Library

Typeset by Avon DataSet Ltd, Bidford on Avon, Warwickshire
Printed and bound in Great Britain by CPI Group

For Christian

January

JANUARY 1ST

Q. What do you give the fifteen-year-old girl with no social life?

A. *A diary!*

Looks like someone did their Christmas shopping in the Ironic Gifts Department this year, eh, Gran?

Happy New Year!

JANUARY 5TH

First day back at school after the Christmas hols and things were not great.

Actually, that's such a massive understatement, it's probably visible from the moon, like the Great Wall of China. Or Graham Flett's arse.

Bumped into Fat Flett on my way to karate last night, so at least I was expecting combat-themed 'banter' from him and his twatty mates on the bus this morning. And I certainly got it. Yep, a whole twenty-five fun-packed minutes of 'Behold the Ginger Ninja!' and comedy karate chops.

Hilarious.

But, as everyone knows, an MP3 player is a bullied girl's best friend and that's why my iPod is my God. Music–1 Abusive Boys–0.

The bus pulled up and, after one last *chop suuuuuey!* from some random lad, they all swarmed off to their school and I escaped into mine.

Molly and Mikaela were already in registration, verbally stirring the cauldron of bitchiness. *Maybe they'll pick on someone else? Just for once?* No chance. The word 'Lara' floated over and my suspicions were confirmed: today was *definitely* going to be a Bleak Day.

When break came, Mrs Muirhouse turfed me out of the cloakroom where I'd been cosying up to a friendly radiator. So, there I was, shivering to death on my own in the yard when the witches of form 11G materialised before me.

'Hi, Lara,' said Molly in the warm, friendly manner of a talking shark. Immediately my hackles rose. (Metaphorically that is. Physically, I'm not sure I even have hackles.) 'I wanted to tell you I spoke to your mum yesterday when she came to clean our house. Did you know she's started working for my parents?' Cue sycophantic laughter from Mikaela. 'Weird, isn't it? Next time I'm in my new en suite doing, whatever, I'll be thinking of *your mum*.'

'Lara's mum's a scrubber!' shouted Mikaela and they all fell about laughing.

Mikaela Walker, you are a comic genius. I. Literally Split. My. Sides.

Of course, a *true* Ginger Ninja would have pulled herself up to her full five foot ten at this point and obliterated Molly with a killer windpipe chop. But I couldn't even manage a killer one-liner. *Hopeless.*

Former Best Friend Forever Chloe-the-Turncoat crept over when Molly wasn't looking.

'Hey, Lara.'

'What do you want?'

'Just saying don't let Molly and Mikaela wind you up.

Being a cleaner is nothing to be ashamed of. Honestly. I mean, it's not like she's a *prostitute*.'

???!!

'Anyway, don't take it personally, they're only having a laugh.' And with that she snuck off furtively, like she was being tailed by the FBI.

What a total hypocrite she is. *Prostitute!* She's known my mum since we were in reception.

Oh, Chloe Stubbs. We were like sisters, you and me. Years and years of best friendness at primary then ecstatic when we both passed the girls' school exam. Inseparable at guides / pony club / karate and then, halfway through Year 9, *poof!* you vanished. No more hanging out at school, no more clubs.

No more being best friends.

Looking back, the signs were there, I just didn't read them: ignoring my texts; not picking up when I rang; disappearing every dinner time . . . I bet the whole class was laughing behind my back for weeks.

Never been dumped by a boy (as never had a boyfriend), so I don't know if that's worse, but being chucked by your best friend is preeeetty gutting. Particularly when she ditches you for someone as mind-meltingly inane as Molly Hardy-Jones. No kidding,

I've had *socks* with sparkier personalities.

Even now I find it mystifying that Chloe turned into this gold-digging airhead. Molly clicked her (acrylic gel-tipped) fingers and my best friend gave me the elbow quicker than you can say 'check out my new en suite'.

Anyway, Mrs Murphy took pity on me at dinner, letting me do some shelving in the library which meant I didn't have to brave the yard again. But it was BIG LAUGHS all round at the bus stop later so v. glad I had my iPod to drown their stupid voices out.

Yeah, so my mum's a cleaner. Big effing deal. At least she works for a living, unlike yours, Molly, who despite being a lazy, sorry, *lady* of leisure, can't be bothered to get off her bony backside to pick up a duster once in a while.

These are tough times. It wasn't Mum's life goal to be a cleaner, but after the business went under, it was that or starve. Seriously think she and Dad aged about ten years in six months. And not just because the business flatlined. Selling the house was definitely the lowest of the low points. Standing on the drive in a family hug; Simon not really getting it; Mum trying to act brave; Dad promising it's only temporary.

But two years later it looks pretty permanent to me.

And that's why, far from being ashamed of her job, I am actually *proud* that my mum cleans your house, Molly Hardy-Jones. Because when she picks your skanky knickers up off your bedroom floor, she is doing it to keep me, my dad and my brother going. Meaning she is a star not a scrubber.

So screw you, Molly Hardy-Jones, and your new en suite. My mum is the Queen of Clean and she rocks her rubber gloves like a GODDESS. And if you EVER leave your dirty pants lying about for her to deal with, I swear I will stuff each and every pair in your big fat gob.

PS Molly's got her own en suite. Me and Simon share a flannel. There literally is no justice.

JANUARY 8TH

Simple Simon (aka World's Dumbest Kid Brother) stuck a knife in the toaster and ripped its guts out while I was making the tea tonight. *Then* he tried to stick his tongue in a light fitting, blowing all the fuses in the house (including Dad's), which meant when Mum got in from work, the three of us were a) starving and b) blundering about in pitch-darkness.

Never mind 'ass', Simon is an omni-pain in the brain, body and soul. He surpassed 'ass' at about eighteen months. Hard to believe it now, but when he was first born I *loved* playing Big Sis. Taking him out in his pram, blowing raspberries on his tummy, dressing him up like a doll.

Ha! How times have changed. He has belonged to Satan since the minute he learned to talk. No matter how much I threaten him, his mouth is ALWAYS on full volume while his brain's turned way, way down. And the little freak constantly gets me into grief.

Like tonight: instead of dealing directly with her delinquent spawn, as any normal mother would, Mum had a right go at *me*.

We are currently stuck on a loop, like that film *Groundhog Day*, except ours is called *Everything is Lara's Fault Day*. OK, Mother, totally get you work hard, are sole breadwinner, etc., but STOP TAKING OUT YOUR MOODS ON ME.

Tonight's variation on the theme: beef Hula Hoops.

'What's this all over the carpet?'

'Could be Hula Hoops. Simon had a packet earlier.'

'First the electric's off and now the place is a pigsty,' Mum snapped. 'I am sick to death of coming home to this every night.' She poked at the crumbs with her foot. 'Look! Right the way up the stairs. It's like sharing the bloody house with Hansel and Gretel.'

'Er, yeah, they're not my crisps. Tell him, not me.'

'It's your responsibility to make sure things are straight; you're the eldest.'

'That is so unfair. I have to do *everything*.'

'Lara, Simon is *six years old*. And anyway, he does his share.'

!!!!

I clattered the hoover out of the kitchen cupboard and naturally I did tut, sigh and roll my eyes while I was doing it, of course I did.

Simon 'does his share' round the house? What a joke. You can count the number of times Simon's 'done his share' on the fingers of an oven glove.

More to the point, why isn't she nagging Dad to 'do his share'? I mean, if we're getting technical here, isn't *he* the eldest?

I am up at five every day delivering newspapers in arctic conditions, while he's still snoring his head off upstairs. (A job I do, let's not forget, so I can pay for karate and other stuff myself, thus sparing them extra expense.)

Then, after school, I've got ten GCSEs to study

for. With the way they go on about the FINANCIAL SACRIFICES they've made for my education, they should see my exams as the Holy Grail. But no. My parents think *clean carpets* are more important.

Meanwhile, Simple Simon gets away with murder and Dad gets to spend his days brooding on the sofa like some TV-obsessed, housework-shy troll.

He's unemployed FFS, what else has he got to do?

JANUARY 10TH

WTF?! Massive shock in English today. Surely Mrs Gill's idea of a good time in bed is the complete Jane Austen and a hobnob?

Well, apparently not. Turns out she's going on maternity leave till September.

Bombshell though that may be, the *real* headline news is the cover teacher they've drafted in. Imagine Edward Cullen and Mr Darcy rolled into one. Well, that does not even come *close* to the glorious gorge-ness of Mr Ben Jagger. And it wasn't just me who noticed either: the poor guy was nearly knocked to the floor by 11G's collective fake-eyelash fluttering. Even treat-'em-mean Molly tossed her hair extensions so hard I thought she'd dislocate her neck. (Sadly, no.)

Anyway, Mr Jagger kicked off his lesson with, 'Right then . . . OK then . . .' and mucho throat-clearing. But once he'd got past the nerves (understandable given the whole class was eyeing him like a starving dog shown a chop), he was excellent and it was BY MILES the best English lesson I've ever had. He'd prepped this interactive video stuff on medieval Verona that was so absolutely brilliant even Thicky Mikaela was mesmerised.

Plus! Not just English, he's our form tutor too, so pleeenty of opportunities afoot to gaze upon his gorgeness.

Never thought I would write these words, but *I am looking forward to going to school tomorrow*!

JANUARY 11TH

Registration was like being backstage at *Next Top Model* this morning. Obviously, we already had the competitive bulimia and bitching, but Mr Jagger's sudden appearance has sent the class glamour stakes stratospheric. Some hardcore make-up bag raids were in evidence and I admit I am just as guilty: nearly missed the bus I spent that long trying to de-bush my hair.

Honestly, he could be a top model himself. Tall, but not gangly stick-insect-esque like me, more sporty and fit, with floppy boy-band hair doing a cool this-is-just-the-way-it-goes vibe, not a posing-in-front-of-the-mirror style. His eyes are amazing too, light green with brown flecks in (*think* so anyway – I need to confirm via a closer look) and a tan like he spends his summers on a surfboard somewhere exotic.

He belongs on a catwalk or the set of an Australian soap. *Definitely* not in a classroom filled with drooling girls. No exaggeration, the whole school is Jagger-struck.

Mr Jagger, Sir: you are a bucketload of glitter sprinkled on a cowpat and you don't even know it. In fact, today you performed possibly the greatest miracle of the twenty-first century: your presence made a day at Huddersfield Girls' High School pleasant.

Well, *almost* pleasant anyway, because the 'your mum's a scrubber' comments kept coming thick and fast. (But since Mikaela started it, mainly thick. Ha ha.)

What can I do? I've tried cultivating deaf-rhinoceros-in-Teflon skin and I've tried answering back, but neither works. If I show a flicker of response, it's like diving into shark-infested waters . . . while wearing a wetsuit made of ham.

Suicidal feeding frenzy.

Rang Emma tonight. Miss her so much. Her moving miles away is the worst knock-on effect of the business folding. More like losing a sister than a cousin. Can't blame Uncle Andy for going though. Nothing left for them here, was there?

Buuut, can't help selfishly wishing Em was still around, especially as the Mean Girls seem to be ramping things up lately. I could do with some local support.

'Molly's always been a bit of a cow. And a complete snob,' she said. 'Chloe will wake up and smell the bullshit soon, don't worry.'

'Maybe . . .' I said, not that convinced. 'How's college?'

She went straight into a rambly story about this 'kick-ass' night out she'd had with a guy from her psychology class. Then how 'awesome' her new part-time job in Topshop is. And how she's going to Florida with Uncle Andy and Auntie Amanda; the new firm is expanding *again* because apparently solar panels are booming in Essex.

So I listened, and really I'm 100% thrilled life is treating her so brilliantly because I love her and she entirely deserves it.

Then, when we'd said bye, I headed downstairs to watch telly. But Mum and Dad were having another one of their hushed rows about money (i.e. lack of) in the lounge. So I made a piece of toast and went back to my freezing, minuscule bedroom, and sat there on my own, feeling sad.

JANUARY 14TH

Newsflash! It's official: Mr Jagger is ABSOLUTELY AMAZING!

Reason 1

OK, so today we're reading *Romeo and Juliet* when he says, 'Right, we're going to do this next activity in pairs. Can you divide yourselves up, please?'

Pairs. The word strikes fear in my heart. Will someone *die* in the scramble not to work with Lara T, Queen of the Untouchables?

And it's not only me. Pairs are tricky for the Weird Sisters: you know — two's evil company but three's a crowd, etc. The word 'pairs' is a guillotine blade ready to drop. Mikaela and Former Best Friend Forever Chloe are visibly panicking. *Who will Molly pick? Who will she choose? Don't pick her, pick me!! Aaarrggghh!*

What they should do is work together and leave Miss Molly flying solo, but they're too dim to see that. Plus it's pretty obvious beneath the besties act that they completely despise each other. Anyway, after a few seconds, Mikaela's lonesome brain cell lumbers to life and she pipes up, 'Sir, how many in each group?'

Mr J managed to keep a straight face while he said, 'Two, please,' in a perfectly normal voice. But he saw me watching him and raised his eyebrows a tiny bit as he caught my eye. Then he kind of shrugged *What is she like?* Entirely, solely at ME. Ha!

Next, when the class (as is the custom in 11G) left me *alone, alone, all, all alone*, instead of forcing me into a group like Mrs Gill always does, he went, 'OK, Lara, you can work with me.'

Got to spend five minutes doing character maps with him and he seemed v. impressed that I knew so much about the play already. The stuff he said was properly interesting AND it gave me the perfect opportunity to confirm that his eyes *do* have amber flecks in them. Amber or hazel anyway. Dark honey-coloured.

That aside, he is so fantastically brilliant at explaining stuff that I learned more about Romeo and Juliet & Co in those five minutes than I have in the last five weeks. (Sorry, Mrs G, but it's true.)

Reason 2

Home-time and I was waiting for the Hellbus, minding my own business, when Molly saw me give my head a totally innocent scratch.

She smirked, shouting out, 'Urgh, Lara, have you got nits *again?*' which was followed by mass shrieks and a stampede as the girls nearest to me fled. At least the boys' school hadn't let out yet, so I was spared that added humiliation.

Of course I don't have nits. For the record, I had them *once* in Year 7 (caught from Simple Simon). But somehow Molly has managed to weave this isolated episode into some tedious non-joke that I'm a walking bug motel.

'I can see them jumping on your head!' she yelled from the 'safety' of further up the road.

'No you can't because I DON'T HAVE THEM,' I called back. But no one was listening; all too busy laughing while I shrank deeper and deeper into my blazer.

Now, if my life was a fairy tale, I'd write here that a handsome knight on a snowy-white steed galloped up, swept me into his arms and rode me off into the magnificent sunset. But I'm no princess and it was a beat-up silver car with Mr Jagger rolling the window down. Not complaining though: who'd want a horse in this traffic?

'Is everything OK?' he said, instantly drawing Molly straight to the car, a couple of cronies close behind.

'Hiya, Sir,' she said, flashing her teeth, sticking her boobs out and flicking her hair extensions. 'Have you come to pick me up then?'

The others giggled. Not me. I was too stunned she'd managed to do four things simultaneously.

'Nice try, Molly,' he said. 'But no. I wanted to know what's going on. I saw all these people running off and . . . Lara?'

'Oh, it's nothing, Sir. Just waiting for the bus,' I mumbled.

The rest of the girls had drifted back one by one and were watching us. Mr J looked at me for a few seconds longer, then nodded. 'OK, well, if you're sure everything's OK, Lara. See you tomorrow.'

And he sputtered off in his knackered little car, smoke billowing from the exhaust.

Wow! Can't believe he stopped. That is the nicest thing a teacher has ever done for me. None of the others have bothered to step in before. Or maybe they've just never noticed the way people treat me. Not everyone needs a cloak to be invisible, do they?

Molly looked a bit put out, but at least she shut up and left me alone. Then the boys' school came out and a gang of girls made this faux-squeamish deal of not sitting next to me, but bollocks to them. Least I got a seat. Normally it's standing room only. They keep promising us a bus for each school. Can't wait. The girls are bearable-ish, but the boys are industrial-strength knobs.

Anyway, I stuck my headphones in and starting reading a book Mr J recommended called *I Capture the Castle.* But it was hard to concentrate because all I could think about was him turning up out of nowhere at *exactly* the right moment.

Mum and Dad are stressing over the rent arrears downstairs and, as I can't take another ounce of money's-too-tight-to-mention tension, am taking refuge in my room. Again.

Still can't stop thinking about Mr J. He's kind, clever, good-looking, funny, sporty, loves to read – the guy pretty much full-houses my dream boyfriend wish list.

Depressing really. What are the chances of meeting someone my own age like that?

Slim.

And of him fancying me back?

Ha! *Skeletal.*

JANUARY 17TH

Following on from the *gasp!* shocking revelation that my mum is *gasp!* a cleaner, the Ginger Apartheid Movement has gathered momentum and I appear to have now made the transition from mocked-but-tolerated to actively shunned.

The evidence? Registration this morning and a pink envelope appears on every desk. Every girl pulls out a pink glittery card. The room is buzzing. Every girl is giddy with anticipation. Every girl except me.

Why?

Because I am the ONLY member of Form 11G that hasn't been invited to back-stabbing former BFF Chloe Stubbs's 'Sweet Sixteen Celebration'.

(Pink glitter! Un. Be. Lievable. We had matching *PINK STINKS!* badges on our blazers in Year 8!)

Anyone else's party and I wouldn't even be that arsed, but this is Chloe giving me the *unclean, unclean* social leper treatment. And I don't get why; not really.

Yeah, I realise I was never hanging with the cool kids, but me and Chloe got on great until Molly wormed her way between us. Even the girls we used to knock about with like Kayleigh and Eden have drifted over to Team Molly along with Chloe. They're never mean or bitchy, it's more like I don't exist any more.

I am the Invisible Woman.

And the mystery remains: why has Molly got it in for me on such an epic scale?

As far as I'm aware, it's not an actual crime to be intelligent or ginger or have a stupid surname or a mum who cleans (even though Molly seems to think it is). What is it with her? Does she think being poor is catching? *Caution! Friendship with Lara T may result in fatal outbreaks of Primark, Pot Noodles and pound shops.* Stuck-up cow.

And now today's little stab looks like last-nail-in-the-coffin time. *Everyone* gets an invite to the pink puke fest apart from me and the only hint of a silvery lining was that Mr Jagger had a meeting so he didn't witness my shame.

Later . . . Just had a Facebook message from Chloe aka The Traitor.

Hey Lara! I hope you don't mind about the party but I knew it wouldn't be your sort of thing. I did want you to come, honestly, but I think it might be better if we do something on our own another time instead? Love Chloe xx

Get this, right. I am in the middle of typing *No worries! I know you were only thinking of me* when a flock of flying pigs pass over the house and knock the 3G out.

What are the chances . . .?!

JANUARY 19TH

Brrrr! Mum and Dad have announced we're on yet another economy drive, so the heating's off tonight. I want to know exactly what there is left to economise on. We live the no-frills life in our house as it is. Are we going to feed Simon to the dog? Start rationing the bathwater? Hmmm, I'd rather not add 'I stink' to The List.

The *Why Lara T is Queen of the Untouchables* List
- I'm ginger
- I'm poor
- I'm a geek
- I have the Surname of Shame
- My mum cleans for a living

And coming soon . . .

- I stink

Seriously worried I am becoming worse than Untouchable. Is there a lower caste, one even the Untouchables look down on?

Joke: *What did one Untouchable say to the other Untouchable?*
'At least we're not Lara T!' Ha ha!

Anyway, the further 'austerity measures' mean I haven't dared ask about getting a new school skirt, despite the fact this one is almost gynaecologically indecent. Short skirts might always be in fashion, but freezing your twinkle to a bus shelter will never catch on.

Oh, PLEASE don't let us be poor for much longer. When will we be able to afford new clothes? Heating? Fruit?

Hmm. Sounding v. ungrateful bitch-esque here, which I so am not. Am I demanding caviar in a gold dish on my private yacht? *Nooo*. And I am fully aware that

Mum's cleaning and the money left over from selling the house isn't stretching as far as they'd hoped AND that it's my school fees sucking the last few quid out of their savings account.

But I can't help pining for how it was before everything went down the toilet. Dying to have the little things again. Satellite telly, weekends away, family trips to the cinema, clothes shopping . . . the stuff I completely took for granted.

Stuff we could probably still have (now and then) if it weren't for the FINANCIAL SACRIFICES they make because we have to keep Genius Lara at her Good Private School (the irony!). Mum, Dad and Simon — we'd *all* have better lives if it wasn't for my stupid school fees which, even with the 50% braniac bursary, are astronomical. Wasn't easy to pay when we actually had money, but now we're on the breadline, well, it explains the economy overdrive.

And that's why I can't tell them how much I hate school, no matter how bad it gets. Throw the massive FINANCIAL SACRIFICES back in their faces, would you? Selfish, ungrateful bitchcow of a daughter.

Could never confess this to anyone, especially Dad, but I was almost relieved when he and Uncle Andy gave up the fight. Obviously, that was misery on toast, but it meant the tension stopped – that horrible scrabbling on a cliff edge thing with the pair of them constantly up and down to the bank, begging for more time. Once they'd given up and the house had gone to pay the debts, at least the uncertainty was over.

I may actually cry if I think about this much longer. Soooo . . .

Yay! (drum roll) The weekend has arrived at last, full of thrilling possibilities: parties, premieres, paper rounds . . .

Thank God no one has any of the Sunday whoppers round here, I can barely lift the bag as it is. I bet Molly's parents get *The Times;* they probably order five copies and spring-load the letterbox just to taunt their paper girl.

Not that Molly could actually read it of course. She's far too dumb.

JANUARY 22ND

Karate was excellent tonight and I cannot wait for the day when I Jackie Chan the bejesus out of everyone who annoys me at school. *Hiiii yaaaaah! Chop.*

Went round to Gran's after with the shopping and had a cup of tea. She did wake up briefly for the Sky Sports headlines, but mainly I ate choccy digestives and broiled myself on the central heating. Mmmmm, warmth: how I miss you, old friend. Mum and Dad are still point-blank refusing to turn the heating on (fuel costs blah bills blah money blah) so only a pair of thermal socks and dreams of Mr J came between me and hypothermia last night.

On a brighter note (hallelujah and praise the Lord), I'm currently enjoying a respite schoolwise because Molly is so *entirely* obsessed with the lovely Mr J that flirting with/ talking about him consumes all her time.

<u>Typical conversation of the day</u>

Molly: I'm off for a sandwich. You coming?

Mikaela: What do you reckon Mr Jagger's favourite sandwich is – egg and cress?

Chloe: No, that's too gay. Tuna salad?

Molly: Salad? No chance. He's a proper man. It'll be ham and mustard, something like that. Hot. Meaty. Little bit spicy.

Aaaand so on.

Gay sandwiches, eh? Who knew?

Ever since Molly had her hamster-to-human brain

swap, when she's distracted (e.g. by sunflower seeds, hibernating, fancying the hot new English teacher, etc.), there are no spare neurons available to monitor other activity. Which means I can slip under her radar for a bit. Not so much as a single ginger jibe all day. Result!

Now if only a fit teacher could start at the boys' school then maybe the bus lot would leave off for a bit too. Tonight at home-time some lad I've never even laid eyes on before was loudly jabbering on in my direction about 'kick a ginger day'. I plugged my iPod in to ignore him, assuming he was making it up, but a quick Google confirmed it later. A dedicated ginger-bashing day does indeed exist. You can even buy commemorative mugs.

How can that be *legal*, never mind socially acceptable? If we've got laws against abusing people because of the colour of their *skin*, why not hair? Blonde, black, brown, bald, grey, red: one nation, follicly united!

Later . . . Oh dear. Dad has just lost it big-style with Themnextdoor (mutual anonymous loathing – we don't know their names, they don't know ours).

They've just dumped (*boom boom*) the dog poo from their yard over our fence. Most of it landed by the car on the driver's side. Dad nipped out to get some fags and, well, the upshot is he's had to throw his best trainers in the bin. Not good: wars have started for less.

JANUARY 28TH

Themnextdoor are driving Dad to new – heights? depths? – of grumpiness because their YAP ratty YAP little YAP dog YAP never stops YAPPING.

I guess it's worse for Dad because at least the rest of us are out during the day. He went round after tea to complain about dog/rat and they just laughed in his face. He got straight in the car and he's still not back now and it's half ten. Mum's rung his mobile about twenty times, but it's switched off.

Better news! There are some exciting potential developments on the Hellbus front in that I have had a Eureka moment. (Except not in the bath and I didn't run down the road starkers. Ha ha.)

Humanity's past glitters with such moments. Ideas so simple yet so revolutionary they've changed the world: *How about if I rub these two sticks together? Is it me, or do we all look a bit like monkeys? Chips AND cheese?*

And here's my own modest contribution. If I ask Mr Patel for an evening paper round as well as the morning shift, beg Mum for a loan (maybe) and use up all my savings, I should be able to buy myself a BIKE.

I know, it's genius. Cycling is cool AND I'll get the papers done loads quicker AND it'll pay for itself in a term as it'll save me forking out for a bus pass AND I'll get fitter AND help the environment, plus (and this is the best bit) I won't need to face the boys' school knobs on the Hellbus ever again.

Go me!

PS 11.35. Still no sign of Dad.

February

FEBRUARY 5TH

Did Mum and Dad win the lottery? No. Has Simon become human? No. Have aliens abducted Molly? Unfortunately not.

Nonetheless, it's been a fantastic day because I got an A* from Hell High's newest and finest member of staff, Mr 'I am so hot I may spontaneously combust' Jagger!

We've been doing some warm-ups for the creative writing coursework. As he's still 'getting to know us as a group', the task to write an essay about the Christmas hols was a bit Year 7, but he is box-fresh teaching-wise (he told us we're his first job), so I'll let him off. Here goes:

My Christmas

As is the tradition in our house, Gran is glued to Noel Edmonds while Mum feeds the stress volcano until she erupts, kicking the oven door. I go in, get some frozen peas to put on her foot and finish dinner off, while Dad sits drinking Baileys (which he doesn't even like) in front of the telly.

By the time The Sound of Music *comes on, our house is alive with the sound of mayhem. Simon's broken his new toys already, Mum's burnt herself as well as all the food, Gran is comatose and Dad's slurring his words. And poor Paddington, our highly-strung golden retriever, is cowering under the dining-room table.*

This year, Dad got even drunker than usual. As we can't afford real Baileys since he lost his job, he was drinking a bargain-bucket liqueur (possibly) called 'Piss'. Anyway, he was plastered and the food was on the table. Mum called everyone into the dining room. When she shouted, 'Lunch is ready,' Gran groaned and Dad, who'd forgotten she was there, jumped up with a scream.

It frightened the dog so much she shot out from under the table to protect him. And by 'protect him' I mean 'leapt up and sank her teeth in his butt cheek'.

Dad screamed again, fell over backwards and went straight through our glass-topped coffee table. Mum went ballistic.

Dad went to A & E. Gran went back to sleep.

Peace on earth and goodwill to all men? Definitely not in our house.

Mum hasn't stopped fuming about that coffee table, especially since she keeps going to put her tea on it, so the carpet's ruined as well. She's mega-moody now too because Dad didn't get home from the pub till after twelve last night. He had to leave the car there so he couldn't take Simon to school. Mum was livid, especially when Dad said Simon should change to the local primary which tangented off into yet another row.

I am starting to really worry about them. Seems the only time they stop arguing is when they're giving each other the silent treatment. Classic example tonight: Mum said, 'Lara, remind your father to put the bins out, will you?' *While she was sitting next to him on the sofa!* Honestly, they're worse than kids.

Anyhow, back to my happy place. Mr J handed the work out, saying, 'I loved reading these; really entertaining stuff. It'd be great to share a few with the rest of the class.' Then when he got to me, he went, 'Lara, nothing less than an A* for your heartfelt piece. Would you like to start?'

I turned it over: *Highly imaginative and detailed work, Lara. Well done!*

Wahey!

Then . . .

'Er, no, Sir. I don't want to read it out.'

He smiled. 'OK, that's no problem. Thanks anyway, I loved it. Chloe? An excellent B. How about you?'

My Former BFF didn't need to be asked twice to thrill us with the Fabulous Tale of her Fabulous Trip to Molly's Fabulous Alpine Ski Lodge. Drone drone drone. I drifted off into a very pleasant daydream about the Fabulous Mr J.

Refusing to read mine out still didn't prevent the slurpy ass-kissing noises I got after the lesson (not from him obviously). Molly and Mikaela carried on looking Jagger Daggers at me all afternoon, which was as unpleasant as it sounds, but still definitely worth it for an A*. It's about time we had some decent teachers to make the FINANCIAL SACRIFICES worthwhile.

Later . . . Mr J 'loved' my essay. Yay!

Now, no one's ever going to call me an expert on the male species, but it seems to me there are two kinds of boy in the world:

1. The ones who say, 'But she's got beautiful hair. And anyway, so what? It's only a name.'

and

2. The kind who go, 'The lanky ginger freak's called what???!!! Ha ha ha . . . oh no, I've wet my trousers.'

Boys I have met in category 1: None.
Boys I have met in category 2: All the rest.

Whenever a new boy starts on the bus, sooner or later they put him through the 'guess the name of the beanpole' routine. Today it was the 'kick a ginger' lad from the other day. Someone pointed at me and whispered in his ear. He laughed like a jet engine till everyone was staring, then came over to where I was sitting, picking moss off the churchyard wall, myiPodismygod blocking out their stupid voices like the truly lifesaving invention it is.

Him: Oy.

Me: What?

Him: Is it true . . . (splutters with laughter) . . . is it true (going purple in the face) . . . is it true (nearly choking) . . . your name's (doubled over, almost wetting trousers) . . . TITLESS? (collapses in heap)

Me: No. It's 'Titliss'. Lara Tit*LISS*.

Him: TITLESS!!!!!! (rolling around, clutching stomach)

Did I go all Ginger Ninja on his ass? Did I heck. I walked off, leaving him writhing on the floor like his appendix had burst. Twat.

Decisions, decisions. What shall I change it to? Something anonymous maybe, like Lara Jones. Flash and exotic? Lara Kostyakov. Or posh? *Lara Willoughby-Smythe, delighted to make your acquaintance.* Who am I kidding? I don't even care; nothing could be worse than the T word.

Wish I could adopt Emma's attitude, i.e. be totally unfazed by the Surname of Shame. She could have ditched it by deed poll when she turned sixteen last year, but she didn't, even though Uncle Andy wouldn't have minded. If I asked *Dad*, I'd never hear the end of it.

Imagine if the world was less alpha male, we could've had Mum's maiden name and Lara *Merry's* life would be an endless sunny-day parade of cupcakes and rainbows. Instead I got stuck with 'Titliss', officially the worst possible surname in the whole world for a flat-chested teenage girl. Even Molly Hardy-Jones would struggle to pull 'Titliss' off and she's got massive great udders. The cow.

PS *And* I found out this new lad's name is Sam Short, so you'd think I'd get at least a hint of sympathy, but no. The only person who *truly* understands is poor Tess Tickle in Year 8.

FEBRUARY 14TH

Had some terrible news today: I'm being sued by the Post Office. It appears our postman slipped a disc lugging my avalanche of Valentine's cards to the front door and will never work again. (Ha ha ha. Please excuse me while I die laughing.)

Graham Flett was the last (ahem, only) person to send me a Valentine's card. Yes, Fat Graham 'Hellbus' Flett. It was in Year 8 and it had kittens on it and came with half a box of Quality Street. (I'm sure he *intended* to give me the whole box.) Of course, he makes out it was a wind-up now I'm the School Untouchable, but I don't think it was.

Mr J of course was absolutely inundated.

And shock horror! Sam Short-Stuff and Molly Hardly-Human are now An Item. Actually, probs not *too* much of a shock. It seems so cosmically right that twin demonic minions sent to torment humankind should unite to rule the world. *Mwaaaaahahahaha*.

They had a real old slobberfest in the bus queue over their Valentine's cards. Might as well have put up a stage and sold tickets. Balloons and teddies. Audible snogging. Ugh. Get a room, you pair of dirty slaps.

Bet Molly hasn't told him she gets mega-minging cold sores though. (Cue advert voice: *Herpes – the Valentine's gift he'll keep forever*.)

Heh heh heh.

FEBRUARY 16TH

Jeez, GET OFF MY CASE ALREADY, WOMAN! Mum continues the nagathon about the less than immaculate state of the house. Er, hello? We're not all anally retentive with a side order of OCD, thanks. She reckons, because she pays the rent, my room should meet her hygiene standards. My view is if she doesn't like it she should steer clear. She wants it clean? Then be my guest.

Soooo, written down, that seems reasonable enough. My mistake – and I hold my hands up here – was actually *saying* it out loud. That cup of tea flew across the room like an Exocet missile. Luckily my reactions are superhero issue so I ducked in time, but the carpet is scarred for life.

Me: (shouting) You can't throw stuff at me! That's child abuse!

Mum: Child abuse? I'll show you child abuse, lady, if you don't clear that mess up RIGHT. This. Minute.

Honestly, there is no talking to her at the moment, and I thought it was teenagers who were supposed to be the stroppy ones. *I'll show you child abuse.* She needs to stop being such a mardy-arse, moody mare and grow up; she's making *Simon* look mature. A sentiment I expressed very clearly by slamming the door extra hard on my way out to karate. *Ha!*

FEBRUARY 18TH

Snow. Loads of it.

Some people, i.e. Simple Simon, look out of the

window and see a winter wonderland, replete with possibilities. Me? Sunday paper round from hell. Absolutely awful this morning. It was like *Touching the Void*. Crampons, ice axes . . . the works.

Extreme Paper Delivery.

I tried to get Paddington to come along, but no joy. Man's best friend? Yeah, sure. Possibly if you substitute 'Basket at the top of the stairs' for 'Man'. She just gave me the canine evil eye and headed straight back to the warm. (Or where 'warm' would be in a normal house, as opposed to one occupied by Mr & Mrs 'Put another jumper on and stop moaning' Titliss.)

I had to snap the icicles off the front door to get out, and I don't mean the outside either. My crappy fake Uggs (Fuggs?) leaked and by the time I got back home my fingers were so stiff they wouldn't operate individually. I was forced to jab at the doorbell with my flipper-like hand till Dad heaved his idle carcass out of bed.

Then when he saw me standing there, lips blue, fingertips blackened by frostbite, etc., all he said was, 'What are you playing at? Shut the bloody door!'

Do I want to spend my mornings wearing a hi-vis tabard and being chased by dogs? Of course not. But until I get a proper Saturday job, a paper round's the only option. He should be grateful I'm trying to earn money to ease the FINANCIAL SACRIFICES, especially now Mr Patel's said I can have the teatime round too.

Then barely even thawed to mauve before Mr P rang to say there'd been three calls complaining about wet papers. Speechless!

Just keep thinking bike fund, bike fund, bike fund . . .

Later . . . Excellent newsflash: just got off the phone and, if the Ice Age ends, cousin Emma is coming up to an open day at Leeds Uni, so she's staying here for a few days.

Getting used to seeing her once-every-whenever has been well rough. Being skint/Mum and Dad at each other's throats/Chloe's vanishing act/chucked out of our lovely house – all of that sucks biiiig time, but not having Em on tap is the mouldy cherry on the top.

In my fave boring-lesson-avoiding daydreams for the future, I've got a flat with Emma in some glamorous part of London. It's in a Georgian townhouse with black-and-white marble tiles in the entrance hall. My room has high ceilings and sash windows that rattle a bit in the wind, but I don't mind. There are red geraniums in pots on the window boxes and the friendly gay neighbours leave home-made muffins on the doorstep, romcom style.

My boyfriend (who is a dead ringer for Mr Jagger) is coming over to take us to a champagne bar so I'll have to iron the Vivienne Westwood in a minute. We've got a mad night's partying lined up to celebrate Em's new job at Alexander McQueen.

Meanwhile, back home in Huddersfield, Molly Hardy-Jones has also landed her first job: serving on the counter at Greggs.

FEBRUARY 20TH

Guess who Mr Jagger has personally selected to help him on his new 'special project'?

Yep, none other than good ol' Lara T, Queen of the Untouchables!

I know!!! *Blimey.*

Last lesson, I was packing my English stuff up when he asked me to stay behind. Then, when everyone else had gone, he leaned against the edge of his desk.

'Thanks, Lara, I won't keep you long. Now I know Mrs Gill always puts a play on at the end of this term, but I fancied doing something different. A talent contest, maybe, get the boys involved too. Something to get both schools buzzing. What do you reckon?'

'Sounds good, Sir.'

'Really? Not too clichéd?'

'No, Sir. I think it's a good idea.'

'Great. Well, I'd love you to get involved; I think you'd enjoy it.'

Hmm, pretty certain that was the gist anyway. I was too busy contemplating his unearthly gorgeousness to register the individual words. He's got the whitest eyeballs I've ever seen; they glow like Simon Cowell's teeth.

'Er, not sure what I could do, Sir, I haven't got any talents.'

'Oh, come on, of course you have.'

His eyes crinkle up at the corners when he smiles and the amber flecks are like pebbles in a rock pool. (In the Caribbean, not Skegness.) Incredible how not one aspect of his entire being is less than perfect: he looks airbrushed even close up.

'Come on, it'll be fun.'

'I'll think about it, Sir. Thanks for asking me.'

I had to pelt it to make the bus, but it didn't matter because Mr J wants me – ME – to help him!

And while on the topic of unrequited adoration, Themnextdoor's dog has developed a crush on Paddington, attempting (rather ambitiously for a Yorkshire terrier) to hump her at every opportunity. Dad went mental over it last night and turned the hose on them both, icing the drive like a bobsleigh run in the process. How Mum laughed as she went flying.

Then when I went to fill the kettle after the early papers this morning, Dad was already sitting at the table, staring down at a pile of brown envelopes, none of which looked like they contained good tidings. The top one had my school crest on it.

I put on a phoney American accent. 'Who is this Bill guy anyway, and why does he always want our money?'

'Not now, Lara,' he said, without looking up.

I turned the tap off and went to school. Can't even remember the last time I saw him smile.

FEBRUARY 22ND

Bugger. I think I may have made a HUGE mistake. It seems I have made Sam Short my mortal enemy.

'What's this then? The original Ginger Minger?' he said, ostentatiously looking me up and down as I waited near the bus queue at home-time.

I put my headphones in and walked off to hide behind the churchyard wall in the hope he'd lose interest.

No chance. He planted himself slap in front of me, gang of henches hot on his heels.

'Hey, I'm talking to you.'

I unplugged myself reluctantly. 'What do you want now?'

'Did you know you're the definition of ugly, Titless? It's true. I got a dictionary, found the word "ugly" and your picture was right next to it.'

Now what I *should* have done is let his insults blah blah blah over me until he got bored. But I was so pissed off (I don't even know you! Why are you doing this?) that what I did instead was break the Golden Rule of the Bullied and open my BIG MOUTH.

'Have you finished? Only I don't care, so you may as well leave me alone and go and pick on someone who gives a toss.' I faked a yawn for added *yeah, whatever*.

'Oooooooooooo!' chorused the others behind him.

His evil little eyes lit up. 'Well, you should,' he continued. 'Give a toss, I mean. Because you're that ugly you're making me feel sick. In fact . . . *eeeurrgggghhhh*.' He mimed throwing up over my shoes. 'Seeing your ginger face every day is making me ill. You know what, I bet your mum took one look at you in the hospital and wished she'd had an abortion.'

Gobsmacking.

Even some of his buddies looked taken aback by that and I was speechless for a few seconds. But then instead of staying quiet and walking off (sensible option), I carried on not only digging my own grave, but picking the flowers, talking to the vicar and writing the eulogy (metaphorically speaking).

'My face makes you sick? That's a surprise.' I stretched myself to tower over him. 'I wouldn't have thought you'd be able to see it from all the way down there. Oh, and have you seen those adverts for that shampoo, *Head and Shoulders*? Because you need to get yourself some, Snowflake. Top of your head looks like the summit of Everest.'

I wiggled my fingers to mime snow falling and the others cracked up.

Sam leaned in so close I could smell his breath. Honestly, it was so rank my nose nearly fell off. Like he'd just eaten a tin of dog food. How can Molly bring herself to snog him? Dis. Gus. Ting. In fact, how can she fancy him at all? I know he's supposed to be some premier league superstar in the making or whatever, but still . . . repulsive.

'You are *so* going to wish you hadn't said that, Titless. See you around, you scrawny ginger slag.'

Realised with the tiny beginnings of an *oh shit* sinking feeling that he was actually *rigid* with rage.

'Looking forward to it, Short-arse,' I answered, more confidently than I felt, and walked off to sniggers from the other lads and echoes of 'short-arse'.

Around the corner, out of sight, I slumped against the wall, shaking like the big fat wuss I really am. And now, hours later, I can't sleep because I can't stop playing it over in my mind like a horror film. I feel sick, sick, sick to my stomach.

You are so going to wish you hadn't said that.

Well, he was right there.

Why the hell did I open my big stupid mouth?

FEBRUARY 23RD

I am not thinking about yesterday. Not thinking about it AT ALL. La la la. Have got my hands over my ears. Refusing to think about Sam or what he might do. La la la. Instead, am focusing on:

44

My Bus Stop Action Plan

Step 1

Start waiting by the churchyard until the last minute, then sprint for the bus.

Step 2

Sit/stand near the driver.

Step 3

Save all money from both paper rounds to get bike quicker.

Step 4

Stay positive.

Step 5

Stop listening to Dad's Morrissey albums (see step 4).

Mr Jagger collared me again about the talent show idea. He was wearing a white shirt that had come untucked at the back and rolled up his sleeves so his tanned forearms were showing. He looked incredible, he sounded lovely, he smelled *amazing*.

'Look, I'm not expecting you to get up on stage if it's not what you want. But what I do need is a PA-type person because I haven't got time to do it all on my own. Someone sensible that I can trust to do a good job. You're the first person I thought of, Lara. You'd be perfect.'

'What would I have to do, Sir?' I asked.

'Oh, signing up the contestants, the publicity, the running order, ticket sales, stuff like that. We can work it out together.'

'OK,' I answered, sort of listening, discreetly inhaling.

Sniff sniff.

'Great. We'll arrange a time to sort the details out later. Would you like a tissue?'

I muttered, 'No thanks,' and scuttled away.

Blush-a-rama.

Every time I speak to him, I make an idiot out of myself. Oh God, I wish I was *normal*. But I've worked him out now. After witnessing Molly's nit nonsense at the bus stop, he's set himself a mission to Integrate the Outcast. Maybe he did a module on it for his PGCE: Freak 101.

Beyond humiliating.

Buuuut . . . on the positive side, the thought of extra time with him doesn't exactly fill me with horror. Plus Molly will explode when she finds out he asked me and not her.

Result!

Form time, lunchtime, lesson time, all the time . . .

zzzzzzzz. Chloe's gaudy, girly glitterfest has been the SOLE topic of 11G conversation for the past few days. I genuinely cannot begin to describe how THRILLED I am not to have been invited to that party. Today they were going on about spray tans. Come on! It's February and we live in Huddersfield, we're *designed* to be mauve; it's the Pennine gene.

Not for Molly 'tangerine dream' Hardy-Jones though. Mum told me they've got a tanning booth in their garage. Every Saturday morning, Molly and her mum put paper knickers on and spray each other the colour of chicken tikka.

This is the girl who thinks *I'm* weird.

FEBRUARY 24TH

Hmmm, surreal conversation with Mum at teatime.

I'd just got back from picking up Gran's washing and I was telling her about Gran moaning because I'd bought ginger 'denture wrencher' biscuits again. (Her words.)

Anyway, Mum went, 'That reminds me. I was telling Mrs Hardy-Jones how good you are with your gran. How you do her shopping and washing and watch Noel

Edmonds with her and that. And it got me thinking. Molly seems a nice girl . . .'

She paused while I choked to death on my fishfinger.

'Do you ever hang out with her at school? Only you don't say much about your friends nowadays. I haven't even seen Chloe for ages.'

My internal monologue went like this: *Firstly, I don't have any friends, not even Chloe. And secondly, FYI, Mum, Molly is 'a nice girl' in the same way Hitler was 'a real sweetie'.*

'You know, she's always asking questions about you, asking how you are, what you've been up to.'

Sirens went off in my head. *Whoop! Whoop! Whoop! Danger danger!*

'What have you told her about me?'

'Nothing really. Er . . . about karate and your paper round, how much you help out with your gran, that sort of thing. She's a nice, friendly girl showing a polite interest. You'd do well to take a leaf out of her book, you know, make yourself a bit more Peer Sociable. It's not norm– I mean, it's not *good* for you to spend so much time on your own.'

'Peer Sociable'?!

God help us, she's been on Netmums again. I wish she wouldn't do that. It's embarrassing enough to feel like a friendless loser without your own mother underlining it for you.

'I don't know where we'd be without the Hardy-Joneses at the moment,' she said, concluding the Conversation I Did Not Want To Be Having with some more unwelcome info. 'That cleaning job has been a godsend.'

Beholden to my orange-skinned nemesis? The thought was so stomach-churning I couldn't face pudding. I had to give mine to Simon. *And* it was trifle.

Mum never mentioned Chloe's party, so I assume Molly didn't divulge that particular kick in the teeth. But it's a never-ending source of fascination at school. The itinerary, the timings, the venue(s), the clothes, the hair products, the co-ordinated toilet roll . . .

Now the entire class (barring yours truly) has booked in at FunkyFeet for a fish pedicure. Fish pedicure! Jeez. Praying a rookie shoal strips them down to the bone. Chomp chomp. Please, please, Divine Fish God, make it happen.

FEBRUARY 26TH

Taaa-daaaah!! I can now declare the Bus Stop Action Plan a success. No major incidents, just a little mild verbal abuse, but nothing I couldn't fend off with headphones. Anyway, won't be long now till I can bid a cheery 'So Long, Farewell, Auf Wiedersehen, Eff Off' to the Hellbus because the evening paper round starts on Monday. And as I've already got nearly £30 in the kitty plus Mum's donating her Clubcard points (which is so nice of her because I know she wants a new frying pan) I should have enough for the bike by the end of the month.

AND IT'S HALF-TERM!!!!!

PS Found out Dognextdoor is called Beyoncé. No kidding, he really is.

FEBRUARY 28TH

Happy days, oh happy happy days! A fabulous abuse-free NINE of them to be precise. Well, school abuse anyway. Can't comment on Mum and Dad who are both ratty as anything. Sadly, that goes hand in hand with no sign of the godlike Mr Jagger for days, which means my half-term cake is plain sponge, slightly stale, no icing.

Sob.

In other news, tonight Simon did his sowing-crumbs-across-the-carpet thing literally a nanosecond after I'd hoovered the front room. But when I *entirely justifiably* smacked him round the head, *I* got shouted at! Pointed out this was a gross miscarriage of justice, but Dad stropped off mid-rant, tutting as he went.

When Mum got in, I tried telling her what happened, but I only got as far as, 'Mum, while you were at work, Simon –' before she interrupted.

'I'm not interested, Lara.'

'That's not fair!'

'Well, life's not fair. I've enough on my plate without you two bickering. Sort it out between yourselves.'

At least Emma'll be here soon. Finally, someone who doesn't act like I'm a big fat slug in the garden of life.

Oh yeah and Mum? Next time, before you lose your rag over Hula Hoops on the stairs, try and remember:

LIFE'S. NOT. FAIR.

March

MARCH 2ND

Epic battle waging in my head *re* text from Chloe:

Hi Lara, just wondering if you fancy going to Costa tomorrow afternoon? X

Pride: Don't accept the crumbs off her table. This is guilt cos she hasn't invited you to the party.

Boredom: But I'm so fed up of being stuck in the house.

Pride: Go to the library then.

Optimism: But what if she wants us to hang out again?

Hmmm, what to do, what to do.

No money; nowhere to go; can't be bothered with TV; not in the mood for starting my holiday work; ditto going for a run. Only thing I've done all day is take Paddington for a walk so she could chase little kids and make them cry. (Her idea, not mine.) I spent the afternoon apologising to stony-faced parents.

When we got home, Beyoncé launched another canine ambush, hurtling at us like an insane mop head on castors. I (politely) asked Themnextdoor to come and get him, but they just shouted 'posh cow' over the fence and cranked the music up.

Poor Paddington was going mental. In the end, I had to physically restrain Beyoncé with the yard brush, but then he started humping that instead. Hard to tell where one ended and the other began really. All the yelping brought Dad out and he got in a right slanging match:

Dad: For the last time, keep your bloody dog out of our garden.

Themnextdoor: *Obscene word* off you *obscene word*-ing *obscene word*. Our Beyoncé can do what the *obscene word* he *obscene word*-ing likes.

Dad: Bunch of *obscene words.*

Watching Dad have a pop at them was probably the highlight of my day. I don't think it was the highlight of his though, judging by the way he kicked Simon's snowman over afterwards. All in all, not much of a bright spot really.

So I think I will text Chloe back to say yes after all. Perhaps she's finally seen Molly for the shallow bimboid she is. Fingers crossed. It'd be good to have her return from the Pink Side.

But even if it's to say sorry and plead with me to attend the girly vom-fest, there is NO WAY I am going.

MARCH 3RD

Chloe was tucked away in a corner when I arrived, spooning up the froth from her cappuccino.

'Hi!' I said, pulling off my gloves. 'You been here long?'

'Five minutes, the bus was early. It's cold, isn't it?'

I unwound my scarf. 'Freezing.' I gestured at the counter. 'You want anything?'

She shook her head.

Since when did me and Chloe talk about the weather?

I tried to choose between an almond pastry and a cinnamon swirl to go with my hot chocolate. Both so tempting, but . . . raspberry muffin won.

'That'll be £5.70, please,' the barista said.

£5.70!!!!

I nearly dropped the tray. Mum feeds the four of us for less than that.

'How are things?' said Chloe when I'd settled into my chair.

Where to start?

'Yeah, good, thanks. You?'

'Not bad, same as usual.'

The hum of conversation went on around us in the crowded cafe while we both gave our drinks a stir. Then we both started talking at the same time. Awkward.

'So what do . . .?'

'What have . . .?'

I laughed. 'Sorry. Go on . . .'

'I was just going to ask what you thought about this talent contest thing at school. Are you going to enter?'

Pride stuck its head over the parapet and I couldn't resist. 'Not to, like, *do* something in it, no. But Mr Jagger's asked me to help him with running it, the publicity and that.'

'Really?' she said. 'That sounds good.'

I grinned. 'I know, can't believe he asked me. Haven't made my mind up yet though. Not sure it's my sort of thing.'

'Oh, come on, you're telling me you don't want to hang out with Mr Jagger? Have you completely lost the plot?'

I snuggled down into the armchair; it was a bit like old times, sitting gossiping about boys. 'I don't know. Yeah, maybe I'll do it. What about you? Are you going to enter?'

Chloe looked at her half-empty cup. 'Molly wants us to have a girl band, but I don't think I can face it. I hate stuff like that. Oh yeah, and there's the small problem that none of us can sing.'

'Don't do it then,' I said. 'You don't have to do everything she says, you know.'

There was a pause while Chloe chewed her lip. 'Yeah, well, anyway,' she said eventually. 'I think you should definitely help Mr Jagger out. Molly will be mad he didn't ask her though. You realise that?'

'Hmm, now you're talking,' I said.

Chloe giggled and leaned forward. 'You know she is totally obsessed by him, don't you? Guess what . . .' She stopped and leaned back.

'What?'

'Promise you won't say anything?'

'Promise.'

'Well, she says, when she's having it off with Sam, she always imagines he's Mr Jagger.'

Mr Jagger?! 'Ugh, that is some feat of imagination.'

'I know! She's always telling him how fit he is to his face, but when he's not listening she keeps moaning about having to wear flats all the time. He was *raging* when you called him short-arse in front of everyone, you know. He won't let it go.'

I sat up straight. Chloe starting a Molly bitchfest was promising. 'Bollocks to him. He deserved it and anyway why is she going out with him if she doesn't fancy him?' I said. 'She could have any lad she wants.'

Chloe shrugged. 'I don't get it either. Personally, I think he's a complete dick. But she's dead impressed he got picked for Town Juniors. And she never stops going on about how he's got those trials coming up for the England under-21s. You know Molly: being a WAG is like her lifetime ambition. I'm actually really pissed off about it because she asked his big-head teammates to my Sweet Sixteen.'

At that, the party elephant in the room sat down, instantly snuffing out our easy chat with its big fat 'you're not invited' bottom. Chloe went a bit pink and I self-consciously sipped at my drink. (Which was empty by that point, but I didn't know how else to fill the gap.) We talked a bit more about superficial this 'n' that until her mobile beeped.

'It's Mikaela,' she said, reading the text. 'They're waiting for me. I'd better go.'

Run along, little lapdog.

We said our goodbyes and off she went. Hope it was more than just a half-hour truce though. There was a flicker of the old Chloe still visible under the Molly-clone exterior and it was v. v. v. good to see her.

And ultimate yay! Emma's coming up tomorrow.

MARCH 6TH

Haven't had a chance to write the past couple of days because Em's been up and we have had such an incredibly excellent time, the hols have just zipped by. Went shopping (window for me; actual for her); pictures; coffee; but mainly non-stop talk, talk, talk.

Now feeling depressed she's gone and I'm back at Hell High tomorrow. Hoping Mr Jagger appreciates the *hours* I have dedicated to my *Romeo and Juliet* essay. And that he's set aside a couple of days to mark all twelve marvellous pages of it. He'd better be impressed.

Tragic twenty-first-century lovelorn heroine that I am, I copied his public Facebook profile pic and set it as my PC wallpaper. (Hey, if they'd been techie, Juliet would've definitely had a Romeo screensaver, yeah?) In it he's standing on the deck of a yacht. (Boat? Ship? Whatever. You could write what I know about the life nautical on the back of a prawn.) The open sea behind, his beautiful eyes screwed up a little against the light. His hair looks a bit longer, messier and he's wearing cut-off jeans.

'Are you serious?' said Emma. '*That*'s your new teacher? Blimey, he is a god.'

'Well, yes, he is, but he's lovely too,' I said. 'A really, really nice person. Dead funny and interesting. Kind as well. Really, really kind.'

Emma pursed her lips and looked at me. 'You've got the hots for him.'

'Nah, don't be daft!' I said.

'Lara and Ben in a tree, K I S S I–'

'Shut up!' I said, maybe a touch too forcefully. 'I simply respect him as a brilliant teacher, that's all.'

'OK, OK,' she said, but her eyebrows were wiggling *methinks the Facebook stalker doth protest too much*. And even though she did shut up, I could see she was absolutely thinking, 'obsessive screensaver weirdo'.

Then she changed tack, pointing out how excellent doing the show will look on my CV when I finally apply for a proper job. She also made me promise to speak to someone at school about the whole Molly/Sam scenario, and I said if it gets any worse I will. Maybe. Plus she reckons Chloe will get fed up of 'that airhead Molly' soon enough and we'll be buds again. Lovely Em. She always makes me feel better about stuff.

Typical. The one family member I could ever have a decent conversation with and she moved 300 miles away. And when she's here, in some ways it's worse, cos it shines a spotlight on how lonely I am. I know we've got Skype, but it's not the same as having her in person. Life would be completely bearable if she was here, even if we still went to different schools like before. I could cope with Molly and that lot if I knew I had a friend on the outside.

Mum and Dad must be regretting not moving when Uncle Andy said to. There's not much demand for solar panels up here in Darkest Gloomshire, but down in Little Dunmow they're covering roofs like photovoltaic thatch. But no, that was another one of the parental SACRIFICES to keep Lara at the same school.

Anyway, had the best time I've had in ages with Em, loads of laughs. She brought me some of her old clothes too, including a longer school skirt. (No more icy draughts whistling up my foof. Hurrah!) She gets a discount from Topshop with her job and she said she'll keep an eye out for me so, at last, unembarrassing clothes may come my way.

Shopping Titliss-style (spot the oxymoron) currently means Mum chucking any tat that says 'sale' on it in the trolley. Polyester tribal-print halter-neck anyone? No, me neither. There's a reason why these things end up in the sale, Mum, and it's because no one sane wanted to buy them.

Anyway, Em's had to go back for college. And now I am alone. Again.

MARCH 7TH

Who snogged who, wore what, fell out with who, the stretch limo hired by Chloe's dad, the amazing venue, the best night ever had by anyone ever since the dawn of time, et-effing-cetera. Yep, back to school today for an excruciating, real-time bore-gasm over the party.

Yawn.

The only person who didn't witness it first hand was me and I'm *so* far from being interested that I've spent the whole day hanging out on Planet I Really Don't Give A Toss. Obviously devastated to learn the spa fish didn't go for the free human sushi, but not that surprised: even a starving piranha would turn its mandibles up at Molly's manky trotters. Glad it went well for Chloe, despite her traitordom. Very well in fact, as rumour has it she got it on with Rob, Sam's bezzy mate from football. The gatecrashers clearly weren't so unwelcome after all.

Last lesson was geography with evil Mrs Muirhouse who is a) utterly witchy and b) utterly, utterly boring. Her mouth opens and twenty-one pairs of ears slam shut; classroom to coma ward in three seconds flat. But at least Thicky Mickey was there to provide the entertainment with another dumbo classic, namely: 'Is spring the one before summer, Miss?'

Muirhouse the Merciless leapt in for the kill. 'I cannot believe my ears, Mikaela Walker. Were you raised by wolves? In a bubble? On the *moon*?'

I couldn't help it, I had to laugh. Oops, naughty, naughty Lara. Molly lasered me with the death glare and I could sense those evil piggy eyes drilling into me for the rest of the lesson.

Went to take Gran's clean washing round tonight. I opened the door and found her slumped, drooling, in the armchair, her glasses in her lap. No kidding, I was dialling 999 when I noticed the (empty) gin bottle on the floor. So I dropped the laundry bag off, took her teeth out and went on to karate.

PS Mr Jagger is on a training course today and tomorrow so I couldn't even hand my essay in. Pah.

MARCH 8TH

Oh God, Mr J, where were you when I REALLY needed rescuing?

I didn't stand a chance. They ambushed me outside the gates at four o'clock, chucking the Bus Stop Action Plan straight out of the window. Molly's face was screwed up in outrage as she stepped in to block my way.

'Why did you laugh at Mickey yesterday?'

'I didn't. I mean, I was laughing at what Mrs Muirhouse said, not at Mikaela.'

'That's not good enough,' she answered. 'How dare you laugh at anyone. Look at the state of you!'

'Yeah,' added Mikaela. 'You think you're so clever,

but everyone knows you're a freak show.'

'Whatever.' I went to put my headphones in, but Molly grabbed hold of my jumper, bunching it round my throat. 'Hey! Get off!'

She laughed and pulled it tighter.

Chloe tapped at Molly's arm. 'Come on, Molly. Leave her alone.'

'You heard what happened today, Chloe. Titless made Mickey look really stupid in front of everyone. Are you seriously going to let her get away with doing that to *your friend*?'

She said the final two words slowly and deliberately, and Chloe looked uncomfortable.

'Yeah, well, I'm sure it was just a joke. And I'm worried someone might see and . . . that's all . . .' She tailed off and started to walk up the road.

As Molly's grip slackened, I saw my chance and tried to make a run for it.

'Oh no you don't.' Up to this point Sam had been lurking at the back. I dodged his outstretched hand and he caught the headphones, whirling as I spun round. He tugged sharply and then *crunch!* my iPod was under his foot. There was a second's silence while everyone just looked at it.

'Oh dear,' he said, grinning.

'Serves you right,' Molly said defiantly.

I stared aghast as Sam lifted his foot to reveal it, screen splintered, headphones crushed. Molly jerked me back, scuffling the trampled bits into the gutter where they lay glittering among the dirt and leaves.

'That is IT! I am going to tell Mr Jagger exactly what you've done. That was a present!'

'You wouldn't dare!' said Mikaela, but a nervous note wavered under the bravado.

'I would. I'm going to tell him first thing tomorrow.'

'Oh no you won't,' answered Molly. 'You're not going to say anything about Sam or Mikaela or anyone because ONE word from you, Titless, and I'll say your mum has stolen something out of my room. Get it? My dad'll call the police and she'll get a criminal record.'

'You can't do that,' I said.

'Try me.'

I stared down at my shattered iPod and let the words sink in. *Mum. Police. Criminal record.* Sam and Mikaela were watching over Molly's shoulder while Chloe, a little way off now, suddenly seemed fascinated by her shoes.

'And don't you dare laugh at me again either, bitch,' chipped in Mikaela.

What else could I do? I nodded miserably. It might be some scummy cleaning job to them, but it's my family's lifeline.

Molly wasn't done twisting the knife.

'And now say *I'm a loser*.'

'No!'

She reached in her coat pocket. 'Do you want me to call him right now?'

So I said what she wanted and, you know what? I think she may be right.

MARCH 9TH

I've tried reading, watching telly, going on the internet, sketching. I even took the dog out for a whole hour. But nothing works: I can't stop thinking about what Molly said about Mum's job. God knows what would happen if she lost it; it's the only thing keeping us afloat. Knowing that my family's finances hinge on Molly Hardy-Bitchface's ability to keep her gob shut is playing origami with my guts.

Got a text from Chloe. *Are you OK? X*

Sent one right back. *Thanks. You were a big help.*

Surprise, surprise, still waiting for a reply.

Ironically I do feel sorry for Mikaela. I mean, I'm no stranger to the sinking horribleness of being humiliated in front of everyone. Anyway, it was Mrs Muirhouse I was laughing at, not her. And, OK, Mrs M is vicious as a rabid fox with PMT, but it *was* funny.

I was tempted to tell Mum the sorry story, but since her exile to the Republic of Misery, we only really do frosty silence/screaming argument. And things are bad enough for her as it is without making it tricky with Molly's folks.

Most nights I hear her and Dad having their loud whisper-rows. Always on the same topic: money, or our tragic lack of it, to be exact. Now I won't even be able to put my iPod on when they start. Bollocks.

Really, really feeling low tonight. Normally, I'm so focused on keeping the glass half full that I can get through most things. But I'm gutted it's gone; my shield against all the shit that comes my way on the bus and at home. My iPod.

Sam Short. Bastard. You, with parents so rich they probably blow their noses on tenners, this would be nothing to you. But I've got about as much chance of buying a new iPod as you have of winning Mr Universe. And Molly, you crossed the line today. Call me names and I can live with that; sticks and stones, etc. But threaten my mum with the police? Risk an income my family desperately needs? That's a whole new league of super-evil.

Totally fine with a couple sharing a common interest. What is giving me the shivers is that Torturing Lara Titliss is what S&M have discovered is theirs. Molly has never been *this* bad before: touch of verbal nasty, nothing physical and, yeah, it's not pleasant, but it's dealable. I can cope. But now I'm not so sure. It feels like something in Sam has tapped into the core of Molly's uber-bitch and struck the mother lode.

And I have no idea what to do.

Why is money always at the heart of things? Everything seems to come down to how much (or little) your parents have.

One of the things that helps me through my dark times is thinking there's a light at the end of the tunnel, one that will lead me away from my loser life. This big light called 'university'. Imagine: with a degree, I can get a good job and be able to help Mum and Dad out, give them some of the things they've sacrificed for me.

· Ha. It costs something ridiculous now, like a thousand pounds a day, so what'll it be when it's my turn to go?

I bet even Thicky Mickey will get in somewhere if her parents bung a few quid in with her UCAS application.

At the rate things are going, my folks won't have the money to stick a stamp on mine.

MARCH 11TH

Trying to be positive, but it's hard. Hoping if I keep out of their way at least it might stop the situation getting worse. So I have volunteered my services to gorgeous Mr J. I'm going to help him with the talent show and I let him know I'll be happy to put in as much time as it takes. Ecstatically, tactically happy if it provides me with an excuse to hide till everything's calmed down. (I didn't tell him that bit.) He rewarded me with his main-beam smile (swoon).

'I'm so pleased, Lara, thank you.'

'You're welcome. When should I start?'

He laughed. I love his laugh. 'Excellent, that's what I like to see, plenty of enthusiasm. OK, first step, look at some clips of talent shows on YouTube. You've got internet access at home, haven't you?'

'Yes, Sir.'

'Great! So see what you think, look at the way these

things work and then get back to me with some ideas. We can take it from there.'

Hopefully, between the show and soon-to-be-bike-not-bus, I should be able to avoid Sam completely and Molly as much as poss.

Totally gutted about my iPod. Feel really down.

MARCH 12TH

Well, I can at least *start* this entry on a high: Mr Jagger 'loved' my *Romeo and Juliet* essay. Apparently it was 'undergraduate standard' and made him 'rethink his interpretation of aspects of the play'. I got another A*. Not bad, eh? I knew it'd be worth the effort.

But that little ray of light was well and truly put out by what came later. Fast-forward to 4 o'clock and my good day got flushed away down a swirling toilet of unprecedented awfulness. Molly has got me where she wants me and there's NOTHING I can do.

A gang of bus lads surrounded me on my way to the stop, forcing me round the corner and into the churchyard, well hidden from the road and the other kids waiting at the stop. (And any passing teachers on the lookout for damsels in danger.)

Smashing my iPod was clearly not enough for Sam, who began by scraping a line in the snow with his foot while Mikaela and Molly had a kickabout with my bag. He got a couple of his henchmen to grab me and three others queued up, sniggering, behind Sam. Then the four of them took it in turns to see who could spit in my face. That's right.

Four. Boys. Spat. On. Me.

I was twisting and turning to get away, but they were so much stronger. Sam 'evil midget' Short stepped back and filmed it on his mobile after his go and when they'd all done gobbing on me, he swaggered over.

'Told you you'd regret it, ginger bitch,' he snarled right in my ear. Then one of the lads holding me sent me sprawling with a shove.

The bus eventually arrived, but I couldn't hack getting on it so caught the service bus instead, which took nearly an hour on top of the half-hour wait in the station. I had to dash straight to Mr Patel's to pick up the papers, which meant Mum was fuming as I promised I'd do Gran's tea. Then, because my blazer was covered in their gross slime, I had to wash it in the bathroom sink. No way will it be dry by morning either, so I'm going to have to go to school in damp clothes.

I am totally trapped. Can't tell Mr J or any of the other teachers because they'll insist on phoning Mum and Dad, and how awkward would that be? Mum wouldn't be able to carry on working for the Hardy-Joneses. Plus I can't just dob Sam in without mentioning Molly's involvement. And of course there's the not-so-insignificant fact that Molly could decide to get Mum *arrested* just to punish me.

That cleaning job has been a godsend, Mum said. And now she's so close to losing it and it is all my fault.

Stupid, stupid, stupid me. If I was flexible enough, I'd be kicking myself. Why did I have to go and say that stuff to Sam in the first place? He called me the definition of ugly, so what? I should've let it slide. But no. I had to open my big mouth and lob some pathetic Year 5 standard insults back about his dandruff and his midget-ness.

What a complete moron.

When will I learn that shooting my mouth off only ever backfires?

MARCH 13TH

I wasn't going to bother writing today as I feel far too miserable. But as I can't sleep anyway, may as well get it out of my system. Oh, where to begin . . .

When I climbed on the bus this morning?

OK, so I'm freezing my ass off in my still-soggy uniform when I look up and it's immediately obvious every one of Sam's henchmen is glued to the horror movie he filmed last night. And of course I can't even put my music on (RIP iPod) so am forced to hear their stupid commentaries for the whole interminable journey while Sam sneers over at me.

When the bus finally pulled up outside school, I stuck my elbows out, head down and barged my way through the pack of them, followed by Molly and Mikaela. Ran for the toilets where I locked myself in a cubicle, but the alpha bitch was right behind me, hammering on the door.

'Come out and talk to us, Titless.'

'In the toilet, like scrubber, like daughter,' Mikaela said. God, she's so pointless.

'Come on out, Titless,' Molly said, poking her head under the door. 'What do you think you're going to do? Stay in there all day?'

'Go away. Leave me alone.'

'Leave you alone? You must be joking. We haven't even *started* yet.'

'But I haven't done anything!'

'You're joking, aren't you?' Molly said. 'All that shit you said to Sam. And making Mickey out to be stupid.'

Mikaela spoke right into the door. 'You live on a *council estate*, for fuck's sake. How dare you look down on me.'

The first bell rang and Molly thumped the door again.

'If you can't take it, you shouldn't give it out in the first place. Did you get that, Titless? You need to learn to keep your big mouth shut.'

God, tell me something I don't know.

Their footsteps click-clacked away and the outside door slammed. By this point I was shaking so much I could hardly slide the lock back. I leaned on the row of sinks, taking deep breaths so I could at least make it to registration without a massive crying fit.

Hands up, I confess I'm not pretty in the cute cheerleader mould, but how does long red hair and pale skin make me ugly? And, fair enough, I've never been scouted by a modelling agency, but neither have

I cracked a mirror using only the power of my face. I am 100% NOT a monster, a freak or an ugly bitch, no matter what they say.

Unlike you, Mikaela 'Daughter of Shrek' Walker.

I was still looking when the door creaked open followed by the sound of Chloe's hesitant voice. 'Are you OK?'

'As if you care,' I said.

'Oh, please don't be like that.' And she did look genuinely concerned. 'Of course I care. I'm just in a really difficult position.'

'My heart bleeds,' I said, as bitterly as I could manage.

'Can't you just try and stay out of their way? And stop answering back. It just makes it worse.'

'I'm not the one in the wrong here. Why do you always take their side?'

Chloe sighed. 'Come on, Lara, try to understand. This is dead difficult for me. Sam's COMPLETELY got it in for you and Molly's so obsessed with being a WAG, she'd jump off a cliff if he told her to. If I stand up for you, her and Mikaela turn on me. I have tried, believe me, but I can't do anything.'

'That is so not true. There's loads you could do. You could stop hanging round with her. You could speak up when she has a go. You could sit next to me at lunchtime once in a while.'

You could be my friend again.

'How can I? I'm going out with Rob now and he's Sam's best mate. And my family's going to stay at the Hardy-Jones's house in France at Easter,' she added haltingly. 'My mum's dead excited about it. She's been shopping with Molly's mum to buy new clothes and stuff. And my dad's started playing golf with her dad every Saturday. He'd been trying to get in at the club for ages and Molly's dad pulled some strings and . . . he . . . we . . .'

'Well, I hope you'll all be very happy together,' I said. Her mouth moved, but no more words came out. What more *could* she say? She's made her choice.

'Don't be like that, Lara,' she pleaded. 'I'm stuck in the middle. It's really hard for me.'

'Drop dead.'

I picked up my bag and, wiping my eyes, marched out of the toilets and . . . crashed straight into Mr Jagger.

'Whoops, sorry,' he said. Then he sort of *looked* and his forehead crinkled. 'What's wrong?'

'Nothing.' Unconvincing.

'Are you sure? You look upset.'

'Yes. I mean, no. I'm fine, Sir.'

'You know if there's something bothering you, you can tell me, don't you?'

He put his hand on my arm, halfway between my elbow and my shoulder, and held it gently. My heart started thumping harder and my throat closed up. *I will not cry. I will not cry at your unbearable kindness.*

'I know, but I don't want to talk about it.'

'Has this got anything to do with the other night? I might be able to help, you know.'

Other night?

'The bus stop, when I saw you. You seemed –'

'Oh, that, no. It's fine. Honestly, I'm –'

The registration bell interrupted me.

'All right,' he said, leaving his hand on my arm while he spoke. 'But don't forget I'm always here if you change your mind, Lara. Do you need a couple of minutes to sort yourself out?'

Being freaky-tall means I usually communicate with the tops of people's heads, but he's exactly the right height for me to look straight in the eyes. And I saw real kindness written in them today. Mum and Dad are too wrapped up in their own woes to notice me and Traitor Chloe's made her allegiances crystal clear. But I can tell

Mr J cares, *really cares*. And it is such a massive relief to know at least one person is on my side. Especially because it's him.

'Yes please, Sir. Thank you.'

Then he set off towards the form room and I raced back into the toilets. I quickly slid into the furthest cubicle, locked the door and sat on the seat, arms wrapped round my knees. And then I finally let myself cry.

If I concentrate, I can still feel the imprint of his hand tingling on my arm. More than anything in the world right now, I wish he *could* help. But there's nothing anyone can do. What Chloe's done hurts just as much as being shoved about or spat on or any of that physical shit.

Years and years of friendship thrown in the bin because her dad wants to play *golf*.

MARCH 14TH

Deliberately missed the bus before and after school today. Got into massive bother with Dad cos it meant he had to drive me in as well as Simon which apparently means I 'must think petrol grows on trees'.

Yes, Dad. Of course I do.

If it comes down to pissing him off or facing up to

S&M & Co, I'll take grief from Dad every time.

BUUUUT . . . at break-time, Mr Jagger winked at me in the corridor.

!!!!

Ha, he's never winked at you, Molly, has he? I've spent so much time picturing him naked (well, nearly: for some reason my imagination keeps his pants on, like Action Man) that when I see him, I get dead embarrassed. I went bright red and had to scuttle off.

Just when I thought nothing could ever cheer me up again, Mr J managed. And that is why I think he is incredible.

MARCH 18TH

Yeeeeeeeeeeeeeessss.

Hallelujah and glory be! Those cold, lonely hours of traipsing in the dark, dodging potential sex offenders, psychotic bull terriers, etc. finally paid off because I've saved enough for a bike. There's one reduced to a bargain-licious £99 in the Argos sale so I don't need Mum's Clubcard points after all and there should be enough left over to buy a helmet and lock.

High five me! I know it's a kid thing, but seriously

I could not be happier than if I was five years old and Santa brought it on his sleigh *and* I saw him *and* stroked the reindeer.

Woohoo squared and multiplied by infinity: from Monday, I will NEVER need to ride the Hellbus again. So between that and doing the show at breaks, I can avoid seeing Sam, Molly or Mikaela in any place unsupervised by a teacher. In other words . . .

I AM FREE!

MARCH 19TH

I HEART MY BIKE! It's sooooo shiny and new and barring a heart-stopping lorry encounter, cycling in this morning was a total breeze. Yes, eyeballing death under the wheels of a ten-tonne truck is a Sunday school picnic compared to a trip on the Hellbus.

Mum asked about my iPod at breakfast (during the 'List of forbidden bike activities' lecture) and I had to lie and say I'd lost it. I braced myself for angry, but instead she unleashed the *I'm-so-weary-slogging-my-guts-out-for-you-and-this-is-how-you-repay-me* look, which is infinitely more effective at twisting the guilt knife than any bollocking. Especially now she's got THREE more cleaning jobs (friends of Molly's parents, for added tangled webness) so we hardly get to see her at home. And when she *is* here, she's so snappy she makes Mrs Muirhouse look like Mary Poppins.

Mum and Dad are now communicating solely via Post-it notes on the fridge. *Why didn't you give Simon his dinner money/you never said/yes I did/no you didn't.* Such ludicrous behaviour from the alleged adults in our household.

Good news: fingers crossed, the Mean Girls avoidance plan is working. As an extra precaution, have decided to only go to the toilets during lessons. Not strictly allowed of course, but if you hop about a bit, ask the teacher if there's a mop handy, etc., then they always let you.

Bizarrely, I'm sure I saw Mikaela take a picture of me with her phone in form time, but as long as I'm not actually:

a) being beaten up/spat on
b) having my mum's job threatened or
c) having my stuff trashed

then I can handle pretty much anything. No one's gonna mess with the Ginger Ninja. I am *nails*, me.

MARCH 20TH

Me and Mr J had a show meeting after school which meant we were in a classroom. Together. *Alone*. OK, so the cleaner was clattering about in the corridor, but the school was deserted otherwise.

Very tempted to nip to the loos first to check my make-up, but didn't dare run the risk of bumping into any of the wicked witches so made do with the little mirror in my compact. Dab of powder on my nose, quick slick of clear lipgloss and I was good to go.

Sitting behind his desk with his stripy shirt a bit crumpled, tie wonky and surfer-boy hair all mussed up, he looked like a sixth former and when he smiled at me, my knees went to jelly.

'There you are. I was wondering where you'd got to.'

'Sorry, Sir, I got held up.' *Making sure I was gorgeous for you*.

'No problem,' he said and passed me a folder. 'I've put a few thoughts down here; for the organisational side of things. I was hoping maybe you could look through and tell me what you think?'

'OK,' I said. 'But I've had some thoughts already, if you want me to . . .?'

'Fire away.'

Plans have been buzzing round my head like hyperactive bees all week. Did what he asked and checked out random footage on YouTube to cobble together the best ideas. Despite the chronic palm sweatage, I gave a clear detailed explanation of how I thought we should do it. Colour-themed publicity (did mood boards, think violet and black the winner), a proper presentation on the flyers, ticketing, how the rounds should be organised... the works.

When I'd finished, he started clapping. 'Wow, that's brilliant! So, just to be clear, you and I will organise preliminary auditions after school for two weeks. We decide who's going through. Then we, along with some guest judges, pick eight acts for the final on the Friday before we break up? That's the, er . . .'

'Eighteenth,' I said.

'Right, the eighteenth of April,' he said. Then he pulled a mock-worry face. 'Crikey, that's not long.'

'It's OK, I've thought of that. It's all worked into the schedule.'

'You are fantastic. So then we –'

Tried unsuccessfully to suppress my Cheshire cat grin as I finished off his sentence. 'Have a proper show for the final. Sell tickets to the parents to raise money for charity and invite a panel to judge the overall winner.'

'Are you going to audition as well?' he said, in a jokey tone.

'I'm not going up on stage. No chance.'

'Don't worry, I won't make you sing if you don't want to.'

'You'd have to rename it a No Talent show if you did.'

He sighed. 'You know, it's awful to listen to a bright girl like you put herself down all the time.' He patted the chair next to his. 'Come here, have a seat. I've been hoping we could have a private chat.'

My knee bumped his and the hairs prickled the length of my arms. I was that close to him I could feel his body heat. Or maybe it was the radiator. Whatever. *Hot*. His proximity instantly made my lungs shrink two sizes.

'I look at you and I wish you'd, I don't know, appreciate yourself a bit more. Not let other people make you feel bad. I'm not blind, Lara, I know you're being given a hard time at the moment by some of the other girls. But I can't help if you don't talk to me.'

It dawned on me this was his nice way of getting me to open up about my leper status. Mortifying. *Embarrassment central. Mission divert! Divert!*

'Thanks, Sir. Can I ask you something, please?'

'Of course. Anything.'

'I've been thinking about when I apply for uni. What books do you think they'll have expected me to read?'

His face brightened. 'You're definitely going to apply to do English then? I mean, it's a while off, you don't have to make your mind up yet.'

'Pretty certain. It's my favourite subject anyway,' I answered. *Because of you, Mr Jagger, because of you.*

'Well, I think you'd love it. You seem to get the idea of different interpretations already and that's quite a sophisticated skill for someone your age. Of course I'll sort you out a list.'

Phew. Mission accomplished.

We had a chat about the final details for the auditions show stuff. He was getting enthusiastic about it, gradually leaning in closer and closer as he talked. I could feel him; I could smell him. Then our legs were nearly touching. He kept talking and feeling his leg right next to mine was sending shivers through my whole body. Chest tight; hardly able to breathe. It felt like I was standing on the edge of a very, very high cliff.

My skirt, his trousers: two thin cotton layers away from bare skin on bare skin. Then his leg touched mine as he turned to pick up a folder and I almost passed out.

He carried on oblivious, but I could hardly follow what he was saying.

Bang! The cleaner smacked the hoover against the door and Mr J looked up at the clock.

'Crikey, is that the time? Let's leave it there then, shall we? Thanks for stopping behind.'

He acknowledged the cleaner with a nod.

'You're welcome, Sir,' I said in a huskier-than-normal voice.

'And thanks for all those great ideas.'

'I'm really looking forward to it.'

'Good. And will you think about what I said about the other girls, please?' he said quietly as the cleaner clattered around, turning in the doorway to give us another glare.

I nodded and then he put his hand on my shoulder. 'You've got such a lot going for you, you know. You're a very special girl.'

The cleaner held the door open and I floated out of the room, on to the bike and down the dark streets to home.

Since I was tiny, like every other girl, I've been sold the idea that my Prince Charming is somewhere out there. *Be patient, my pretty*, they tell us, *and your one true love will appear. Cinderella, Sleeping Beauty, SnowWhite, Little Mermaid* and a dozen other Disneyfied tales. Eventually he'll find me, kiss me and take me to live happily ever after in his castle. (With various talking woodland creatures. And possibly a wise-cracking donkey.)

BULLSHIT.

After a few years, the reality sinks in. Some perfectly pleasant girls (i.e. ones like me) can't attract *frogs,* let alone princes, and that's when you see it's all a BIG FAT LIE.

But suddenly, out of nowhere, Mr J *has* found me and he's *exactly* what the stories promised: funny, kind, clever, interesting, gorgeous. When I'm near him, I feel happier than I thought I ever could. He thinks *I'm* special.

And I can never have him.

Mr Patel let me have a bunch of flowers when I dropped my bag off at the paper shop tonight. Nothing special, just the last bunch of daffs he had propped up in a bucket outside, but Mum acted like they were a £50 bouquet.

'Thanks, love,' she said, squeezing me into a hug. 'What's the occasion?'

I shrugged. 'No reason.'

Dad walked in then, just as Themnextdoor started

revving their thunderous quad bike on the drive. He stood motionless, listening, then opened the fridge door and took a can of lager out. At *ten past five*!!

You've only got to see Mum and Dad nowadays to know Life's Not Fair; and I can't see a happy ending to their un-fairy tale.

Or mine.

I've got more chance of shacking up with seven dwarves than having my prince.

MARCH 21ST

Mr Jagger, you are without exception my favourite person on earth, but I wish you would abandon your misguided attempts to 'integrate' me. Seriously, it's the equivalent of trying to put a bonfire out with petrol.

Today: 'A wonderful essay from Lara here. So good, in fact, I want to share it with the rest of you.' He passed the photocopies round the room. 'OK, folks, here's what an A grade would look like in the exam.'

Needless to say, Molly took hold of her copy like it had been dipped in dung. I know he's only trying to help, he's being nice, I should be grateful, etc., but seriously, he may as well have buried me up to the neck and handed out the stones. Molly and Co threw the Jagger Daggers big time, giving it gargoyle-faced evil all lesson.

What can I say? I love English (I love Mr J!) and I love learning new stuff, but Molly seems to think it's a campaign to make her look stupid.

Yeah, right. Since when does she need *my* help to look dumb?

It's not my fault she got a D for her essay. If she invested half as much time in studying as she does in bitching, flirting and preening, she might lift her grades.

'Please don't forget, everyone,' Mr J continued, 'if you want to share your talents with us in the end-of-term show, then you need to register your act with my brilliant assistant, Lara.'

Then he beamed his megawatt smile straight at 'brilliant' me. If looks could kill, Molly's Medusa-glare would've had me on a cloud strumming a lute within seconds.

When the bell rang, Mr J swept out in a flurry of papers and books, and from the corner of my eye, I spied Molly whispering to a few of her fellow Slytherins. Kayleigh and Eden both glanced at me, shook their heads and left straightaway. I crammed my folder in my bag and headed for the door myself, fast as I could, but Molly was quicker.

'I read your essay, Titless, and it's a pile of shit,' she said, crumpling it up in a tight ball. 'So don't start believing you're anything special, he's just being retard-friendly.'

She arced it into the wastepaper basket then airpunched. 'Slam dunk!'

Her little coven of wannabees filed out, each one repeating Molly's actions until the bin was almost half full. Chloe came last. She hesitated, looking at me, then grinned at Molly, screwed the paper up, repeated, 'Slam dunk!' and threw her copy in the bin too.

Ignore them, ignore them, ignore them.

Mr Jagger liked it and that's all that counts.

Definitely all that counts.

Breathe, breathe, breathe.

So that was fairly dire to start with. *Then* Dad went schizoid at teatime because I buttered some bread *sans* breadboard. OK, I get he'd cleared up in the kitchen (for once) but a couple of stray crumbs doesn't exactly warrant a *Crimewatch Special*, does it?

Oops, my mistake, it does.

This Heinous Criminal Act let loose the unabridged

version of his 'Is that what they teach you, eh? At that school? Is that what I get for my money?' tirade.

Obviously, it was on the tip of my tongue to say, 'Oh no, Dad, we don't do sandwich assembly until Year 13. Right now we're focusing on English, French, geography . . . you know, the more academic stuff.'

But as he was wearing a novelty 'boobs' apron and feather-trimmed rubber gloves, I settled for 'sorr-EE' and a flounce upstairs. You can't argue with a man dressed like that.

- Dad's depressed, he doesn't really hate me.
- Mum's tired.
- Chloe's not worth it.
- Molly's a twenty-one-carat jealous bitch.
- Mr Jagger liked my essay and I got an A. That's enough. More than enough.

MARCH 23RD

Risked crossing the playground at break, despite knowing the Mollevolent One would be lurking.

Schoolgirl error.

She raced across, shaking a can of Coke, then

spurted it all over me. Predictably enough, Mikaela was hysterical when I walked into French.

'Hey, Titless! You doing a wet T-shirt? You've got nothing to show, boy-tits.'

'Grow up, Mikaela.'

I sat down, feeling her big bug eyes goggling the evils at me, but Monsieur Canovas came in before she got the chance to say anything else. At the end of the lesson, she passed behind me, hissing, 'Watch your back, freak.'

So, *thump!* Mikaela's face was on the business end of every punch/roundhouse/kick/uppercut/jab at karate tonight. *Kapow!* Watch your back yourself, troll-features.

Brutal, but soooooooooo good.

And today: a miracle! A potential chaos-theory moment. You know that thing where a butterfly flaps its wings when you're (almost) sixteen and a plane falls on your head on your thirty-fourth birthday? Or whatever. This aft in geography, while idly considering marketing Mrs Muirhouse as a non-medicinal insomnia cure, a Year 13 appeared with a message for me. Wah! Summoned to the Head's office. I racked my brain in panic, *What have I done?* But honestly couldn't think of a single thing.

'Come in!'

She was sitting behind a desk the size of Belgium.

'Ah, Lara. Thank you for coming.'

'S'arightmiss,' I mumbled, looking at the floor, hoping the Coke stains spattered across my shirt weren't too glaring.

'No need to look so worried,' she said. 'I've got some good news for you.'

'Yes, Miss?'

'If you would like, I can offer you a place on a two-day taster session at Cambridge University in May, after your exams have finished. One of our current Year 12s has had to drop out and your name was suggested as a replacement. You'll be able to attend lectures; get to know the campus as well as stay in a college. It really is an excellent opportunity.'

I answered, 'Why, yes, of course. And don't worry about booking the minibus, Mrs Ellis. I'm sure Pater will fly us all there in his solid gold helicopter. Rah rah rah!'

Not really.

It is a tricky one. Do I want Mum and Dad to fork out thousands if I go somewhere posh like that? No. Do I think Cambridge would want me? No. Do I think I would want Cambridge? Not sure. Maybe. But on the shiny side, a trip would give me a few days away from my current crap life, which makes it a very, very appealing proposition.

But then, like the chocolatey bit at the bottom of a Cornetto, Mrs Ellis had saved the best for last.

'If you'd like to discuss it, you can talk to Mrs Muirhouse. She has all the details although she isn't able to go herself this year so Mr McGeorge and Mrs Torrens from the boys' school are the group leaders. And fortunately, Mr Jagger has kindly stepped into the breach on our behalf. He's your form tutor, isn't he?'

'Yes,' I squeaked, my heart beginning to beat faster.

'Well, perhaps you could ask him for the details. There is some help available that you may wish to apply for, a small fund for pupils in, um, more straitened circumstances.'

'Thank you, Miss.'

A fiesta of fireworks is exploding in my brain at the thought of it: two whole days and nights away with Mr J!

Pack my top hat and polish my monocle, I'm orf to Cambridge . . .

MARCH 27TH

We had a massive turnout at the show registration. Unsurprisingly, there was a bit of double-taking when some of the contingent from the boys' school realised it was the Hellbus *Mingère Gingère* holding the clipboard, but a fantastic thirty-two acts signed up, all different kinds too, like a proper talent show.

Stuff to Do

1. Organise guest judges. Monsieur Canovas and Mrs Ellis definitely. (Probably Mrs Muirhouse too. Gulp.)
2. Get the running order ready.
3. Sort out music and lights with drama dept.
4. Er . . . write a lot more lists!

Emma rang up after tea and I told her all about it. 'Aw, that's great, Lara. That's exactly the sort of thing you'll be brilliant at.'

I reminded her that I haven't actually done anything yet. It might be a mega-flop.

'You don't have to be so hard on yourself, you know,' she answered. 'Of course you'll do a brilliant job. Mr Jagger asked *you*, didn't he? No one else.'

'True . . .'

'How are things at school anyway. Any better?'

Of course, even Emma only knows the tip of the top of the iceberg since I can't share the whole truth of the Nightmare of Hell High with anyone, not even her. Wish I could tell her everything, but I can't risk her confiding in Auntie Amanda. Not unless I want to put my family on the streets.

'Yeah, OK. Guess what, Mr Jagger's doing a trip to Cambridge Uni for two days and I'm going.'

'Let's see,' she said. 'You've got him for English and form. Spend every minute of your free time on the show, and now you're going away with him. Riiiight. So what are you guys up to this weekend then – choosing the venue or buying the rings?'

Only teasing, but she must be psychic. *Hi, my name's Lara and I'm a Jaggerholic. From the moment I open my eyes to when my head hits the pillow, he is all I think about.*

Not that I told Emma that. I'm not telling ANYONE that.

MARCH 28TH

I've always been a contender, but today I hit pole ₁
I am DEFINITELY the world's weirdest person ..d if
anyone ever finds out what I've done, I will shrivel up
to a withered husk of humiliation. Making me feel a bit
peculiar even writing it down. *Deep breath*. Here goes,
confession time: I secretly recorded Mr Jagger talking in
English this morning.

I know, I know, it's mad and weird and obsessive and
stalkery, but just hearing him say the words *Please turn to
Scene 3* makes my insides glow. I've got headphones in,
lying on my bed writing this, listening to his voice on my
phone. I need therapy! (Although, chiefly I need a less
crap phone. I only get fifteen seconds' recording time
on this prehistoric chunk of junk.) I can't control myself
though; thinking about him is like breathing to me.

Mum's been vaguely approving about me staying
after school to help with the show. ('Vaguely' being
the equivalent of 'hanging out the bunting' in World of
Mum.) Intended to tell Dad too, but he was lurking up in
the loft with his train set and I didn't want to interrupt.
He's been pacing the floor up and down, up and down
above my head all night, like some mangy old tiger in an
undercover documentary. It's gone ten and he's still at

it. What is *wrong* with him? He's hardly ever downstairs nowadays.

Popped in to drop the *Racing Post* off for Gran after I'd finished the papers. (Have I mentioned how much I HEART MY BIKE?) Put her clean clothes away and left her to snooze in the chair. Maybe it'd be better to catch her in the morning, before she's had her 'five a day' (i.e. gin units, not fruit and veg). No mistaking her and Dad are related, eh?

OK, turn to Act 2, that's page 102 if you've got this edition of the book. Now . . .

Loony bin, here I come . . .

MARCH 29TH

Seems like a different lifetime now, but if I really concentrate, I can remember when we were a TV-worthy family: smiley Mum and Dad, two happy kids and a photogenic dog. Camping holidays in the South of France with Uncle Andy, Auntie Amanda and Emma, when the sun shone down on us every day and we had fun, fun, fun.

Life chez Titliss is very different kettle of *poisson* nowadays and I am sick to death of listening to Mum and Dad arguing when they think I'm asleep. Paper-thin walls in rented houses, you see. Tonight I could hear every word.

'Well, if you hadn't used our home as collateral against the firm, then we wouldn't be in "this hellhole", would we, Tony?'

'That's it, go on, blame me. And if you hadn't wanted to spend every penny I ever earned, then we'd have had something to fall back on now.'

'I never asked for anything for myself! I only ever wanted what was best for us and the kids.'

'Yeah, the posh school for Lara. Now what do we do about Simon? We can't afford both, we can't afford *one*. We could've if you'd agreed to go in on the solar panels with Andy. But no. You insisted we had to stay up here and live in this dump. And look where that's got us: up to our neck in debt, being driven up the wall by Themnextdoor.'

'What, so we should've uprooted the kids from their schools? Taken them away from their only security after the roof over their heads had gone? And Lara starting her GCSEs? Get real, Tony. It was never an option.'

Aaaaand so on. Same old argument over and over till Dad finally stomps off up to his beloved train set.

Nothing gets resolved; all they do is blame each other round in circles.

I miss our old life. I miss my iPod; even ten-second bursts of Mr Jagger's soothing tones aren't enough to make it better. No point asking for an iPod or a better mobile though, is there?

In the end, desperate to muffle their voices, I sneaked across the landing to the bathroom and stuffed cotton wool in my ears. At least I've got a chance of sleeping now.

In my super-successful future life, I will buy them an incredible house. No, a mere house won't suffice, they deserve a mansion, a *palace* even. With an annexe for Dad's train set and hot and cold running servants so Mum'll never have to pick up another J-cloth in her life.

Oh, and not forgetting a state-of-the-art dungeon for Simon of course.

MARCH 30TH

Overslept. Didn't hear my alarm go off and woke up in a major panic.

I've gone deaf!

Ah.

Cotton wool removed, I jumped out of bed. As I drew back the curtains, had ominous, sinking feeling: it was totally pelting down and windy as anything. Got blown about like an autumn leaf just doing the papers. Mum didn't need to say the words; I knew I'd be back on the Hellbus.

The driver didn't even wait until I'd got both feet on before he floored the accelerator, flinging me straight into the path of dog-breath Sam Short. (Where do they recruit school bus drivers? Jobs4knobs.com?)

'Well, well, look who it is. Long time no see, Titless.'

'Yeah, where have you been hiding?' Molly asked.

Wishing I'd left the cotton wool in, I ignored both of them as best I could. But the bus was jam-packed with nowhere to go. No escape. Nothing for it except stand there and face them. And Evil Sam wasted no time in letting me have it. Loudly.

'You know what I like about you, Titless?'

This time I kept my flappy gob zipped.

'Go on, have a guess, what do you reckon I like about you?'

I shook my head, determinedly gazing out of the window while my heart beat a rapid *boll-ocks, boll-ocks*.

'What I like about you, Titless, is . . .' he snorted. 'Fuck all, that's what.'

Molly collapsed in hysterics and sniggers rippled down the bus.

'And Titless,' he continued, warming up, 'I've been wanting to ask you, where's your sign?'

My face was blank.

He prodded my chest. 'You know, the sign that tells you which is the front and which is the back.' Big old laughs at this display of wit. *Ha ha.* 'I mean, I know you *say* you're a girl, but you don't look much like one to me. I mean, where are the jugs?' He mimed some groping. 'You know, the fun bags. The *tits.* You've got no tits, Titless. Jabba's got bigger tits than you, haven't you?' Graham Flett, the target of that particular barb and who was standing next to him, nodded gormlessly. 'I bet you don't even wear a bra.'

Sam leaned forward and started tugging at my shirt, pulling it up under my jumper. 'Come on. Give us a look.'

Why didn't anyone try to help me? The henches were leering and shouting, girls as well as boys, while I hugged my arms to my ribs as tightly as I could. As the bus rattled over a bump in the road, I staggered and they laughed. The kids at the back of the bus must've been able to see what was going on, but no one tried to help. Eden and a couple of other girls from my year looked up, but quickly pretended to be busy staring out of the window or messing with their phones. Afraid to get involved in case Sam and Molly turn on them next, I guess.

The more I struggled to keep my jumper down, the harder he pulled and soon my throat was burning from the effort not to cry. I suffered an eternity of humiliation in the minutes before the squeal of brakes signalled we'd arrived and I finally wrenched myself out of Sam's iron grasp. The tide of school-bound kids gave me an escape route and I ran. My only thought was, *Find him. Find him.*

Mr J looked up from his marking as I dashed into the classroom. 'Morning, Lara. How are you?'

'Morning, Sir, good, thanks.' Knowing Molly and Mikaela couldn't be far behind me, I took the notes for the talent show out of my bag and waved them at him, trying to buy myself some time. 'I thought we could go through some of the details. If that's OK with you.'

He put his pen down and pushed his chair out from under the desk. I jumped as the legs screeched on the tiles. 'Of course, fire away.'

Inside, I was a bag of nerves, but tried to act calm

and soon I was feeling more relaxed. It's really, I don't know how to describe it . . . *restful* maybe? being with him. Like when you've had a bad day and you lie on your bed and it's peaceful and you feel your body unwind.

'Here's the provisional running order for the eliminations. I've tried to make it so there's different stuff every night. Look. Skateboard then dancing then singer on Monday. Then Tuesday, singer, magician, dancers . . .'

By now he'd walked round to perch on the edge of the desk next to me. His soap and aftershave smell made me so dizzy I had to fight to stay on task.

'Excellent, excellent work, Lara! You've balanced it out very well.'

'And I've sorted out the equipment too. Everyone who's entered has instructions on how to take theirs on and off stage and to keep the timings right.'

He smiled and the last slivers of stress melted away like snow in the sun. Now I know everyone fancies him because he's young and fit, but that's not why I like him. Honest. There's something special about him. Unique really. I've never met anyone else with it, this invisible glow that means you're happy just to be near him.

Imagine happiness is a virus, well, it's like that: he

infects you with feeling happy. Sounds stupid, I know, but that's how he makes me feel; being close to him is the only thing in *my whole life* right now that cuts through the gloom because when he looks in my eyes and smiles, I can't see the bad stuff any more.

'That is great. Now, have you got the permission form signed for the Cambridge trip?'

'Er, not yet, Sir.' I was a bit surprised he asked.

'You know it was me who said you should go when the other girl dropped out? Didn't Mrs Ellis mention it?' he said. 'I think it'd do you the world of good.'

He suggested me?! 'Thanks, Sir. I'll definitely get the forms done tonight.'

'You'll have to take them to Dawn, I mean, Miss Longbottom, the secretary over at the boys' school. It's a joint trip and they're organising all the admin over there.'

My heart went flippety-flop. *He* wanted me to go to Cambridge! Out of every girl in the whole year, *he* picked *me*.

But then, because this diary chronicles the Almost Exclusively Shit Life and Times of Lara T, the good stuff was over and things raced straight back downhill.

I (stupidly) let down my guard and hazarded a trip

to the loos at break. Someone crept in and yelled, 'Cheeeeese!' and I looked up to see a hand holding a mobile phone disappear over the top of the cubicle.

Then at home-time, the Hellbus crowd were all at their phones because the photo of me on the bog has gone viral at school. Tough to put into words exactly how that makes me feel. At least my skirt was pulled down over my knees, so no sight of anything intimate (thank God) just my shocked face looking up.

Frankly, it's only the thought of the FINANCIAL SACRIFICES that keeps me going to that place. If it wasn't for Mum working her butt off to keep me there, I'd walk away and never go back.

And if it wasn't for Mr J.

I'd crawl over broken glass if it meant seeing him.

Ah, bollocks to it, I don't care if there's a genuine *cyclone*. I am NOT getting on that bus tomorrow.

April

APRIL 1ST

Yes! Fret no more, Mr J, I am definitely joining you in Cambridge. Got the permission slip signed tonight. Technically signed, just not by my parents.

I did *try* to talk to Mum and Dad, but neither of them was in a communicating frame of mind. He was in the loft again, so I poked my head through the hatch and had a fruitless chat with his ankles. (The rest of him was too absorbed in miniature trains to get involved.)

'Can I go on a two-day trip to Cambridge with school, please?'

'Ask your mother,' he said.

Mum was in the kitchen, chain-smoking and passively listening to Beyoncé howl outside. 'Ask your father,' she said absently.

In the end I gave up and forged her signature, which was probably the most depressing thing I've ever had to do. Even a year ago, Mum and Dad would've hugged me to death and told me how chuffed they were. But today both of them were too wrapped up in their own individual misery to even care.

I am starting to realise that the worst thing about being poor isn't wearing crap clothes or having no satellite telly, it's the collateral damage to your family. All the fighting and the unhappiness and the losing hope are destroying Mum and Dad. And I'm scared that even if they won the lottery tomorrow, we're too lost to find our way back.

Took Paddington up to the nature reserve to escape the lead-lined misery box we call home. One hour later and Dad was *still* in the loft; Mum was *still* staring into space in the kitchen. Don't think either of them had actually noticed I was gone. So I went up to my room and did some publicity work for the grand finale, designing the background for the poster. Black pen-and-ink intricate background with a violet colourwash. V.

happy with it. Then, while I was waiting for the paint to dry, started reading *Wuthering Heights* from Mr J's list of books for the taster lectures.

I saw him before registration again today and we got chatting about the trip. He said they won't expect me to have read every single one, but they're books he loved 'when I was your age'. (Which can't be that long ago. I mean, it's his first job so I reckon he can't be more than twenty-two? Twenty-three?) Then he started talking me through his favourites. I've put stars next to them so I remember which they were.

'Have your parents signed the permission slip yet?' he said.

'No, Sir, but I promise I'll get them to do it tonight.'

'Make sure you do. You know I'd hate it if you missed out on a place.'

Eek, eek and triple eek!

And that's why I had to forge the permission slip. How could I let him down?

Got the scheduling details sorted for the rounds and went tracking people down at dinner. Apprehensively, because over-the-shoulder paranoia is so ingrained it's part of my school DNA now. But I was on a mission for Mr J and his confidence in me was a superhero force field.

V. proud I managed to remain cool and professional giving Molly the list of audition times, when every ounce of instinct wanted to jam it up her piggy snout.

'Here you go, Molly, you're up on Wednesday at 4.45. Good luck.' She snatched it out of my hands without a word (naturally) while Mikaela mimed taking a picture and they all fell about. (Must remember to Google 'law against photographing people on the toilet', see if I can get *them* criminal records.) I was a bit shaky, but did it and walked off, relatively unscathed by the encounter.

Anyway, handing out the rest of the girls' schedules was hitch-free. Mr J's getting the boys' school secretary to do theirs, which, I admit, is a relief. Some surprised faces when people twigged Lara la Loser is in charge of the timetabling as well, but you know what? Go me! Mr Jagger thinks I'm the best person for the job and that's all that matters.

Later . . . Cutting and sticking the photo collage to the poster design when my phone bleeped a message.

Unknown Sender: *U r a waste of space.*

Hmmm. Cheers.

I texted back, *Is that u, Molly?*

No answer.

Deleted the text from my phone. Wish I could delete it from my head.

But I know it's just her, playing silly buggers.

Ignore.

APRIL 2ND

Waaaah!!!

If I die tonight then I shall meet my maker a very, very happy girl because . . . Mr Jagger HUGGED me!

Opening night. The curtain rose and as he stepped into the spotlight, my heart thudded. *What will he think of me if it all goes wrong? Please God, don't let it all go wrong!*

Kids from both schools lined the darkened hall, chatting and shuffling about excitedly, waiting for the singers, dancers and magic acts to begin. This was it! Hours and hours of planning and work and now the first audition; my big chance to make Mr J proud.

Or not.

The crush of spectators in the hall was v. encouraging. Think it's safe to say the publicity has been a triumph. Ticket orders for the final are a bit of a worry, i.e. there aren't any yet, but Mr J reckons we should expect that till the final acts are announced.

Anyway, I was pleased with the crowd, but almost throwing up with nerves, watching him there in the spotlight. He didn't look fazed, but me? Definitely not at ease knowing the responsibility for super success or fucked-up failure is heavily on my shoulders.

A group of Year 10 girls just behind me were doing look-giggle-whisper, obviously pathetically fangirling all over him. Wanted to slap them.

'Quiet. Quiet, please,' he said into the microphone. The speakers gave a feedback screech that swallowed the rest of his words and the stupid Year 10 girls laughed. Monsieur Canovas dashed to the control panel and fiddled with the knobs while I wiped my palms down my skirt then turned to give the thumbs up to the first act, who was hopping around next to me like a demented cricket, waiting for her cue.

The hall went quiet as Mr J announced her. 'OK, first act on stage, please. Ladies and gentlemen, allow me to present . . . from Year 8 here at HGHS, Miss Wendy Bolton.'

I gave her a little shove up the steps. Mr J nodded at Monsieur Canovas. Immediately, hi-voltage dance music blared and teeny-weeny Bendy Wendy leapt straight into a frankly astonishing disco/gymnastics routine. A frantic, sequinned blur bounding around like an optical migraine. Made me dizzy.

'Well done!' said Mr Jagger, striding back on when the clapping had died away. 'And thank you, Wendy, for opening our auditions in such spectacular style.'

Wendy, panting and sweaty, took the bottle of water I held out to her and glugged it back in one. Mr J looked down at me holding my clipboard. 'Now, next up we have . . .?'

'Graham Flett,' I said.

Mr J started the clapping. 'Ladies and gentlemen, I give you the one, the only, Mr Graham Flett.'

Successfully disguising my personal animosity, I pointed the fat bastard up the stairs. What a hugely satisfying experience it will be, I thought, to watch the Lord of the Pies make a fool of himself in public. And poetic justice, considering his role in humiliating me.

Jabba the Flett heaved his lard up the stairs, moobs jiggling with each thunderous step. He stomped to the centre of the stage and stood staring at the audience as if he wasn't quite sure what he was doing there. Then he opened his mouth and began to sing.

Wow.

Angelic notes soared and the scruffy hall was

temporarily transformed into a cathedral. Turns out he's a choirboy. Who'd have guessed? Audience stunned to silence and song done, he sniffed, gave his nuts a scratch and thudded back down the steps to a sudden explosive riot of whistles and cheers.

'Er, thank you, Graham!' said Mr Jagger over the applause. 'And I think I speak for us all when I say I honestly was not expecting that!'

Too right. I'd've been less surprised if he'd pulled a brontosaurus out of a hat.

The rest of the acts were more predictable: a mediocre magic act, a nervous gymnast and some enthusiastic street dance. I ticked each one off on my clipboard, scribbling down quick pointers based on the audience's reactions and my impressions.

Mr Jagger beckoned me over once we'd wrapped things up and the hall had begun to empty. 'So what do you reckon? Who are we carrying forward?'

'Me personally, and the audience, definitely Graham and Wendy,' I answered.

'Great minds think alike.' He whipped out one of his knee-liquefying grins. 'OK, put them on the list. We'll let them know next week when we've seen all the contestants.'

I jotted Graham and Wendy's names down as he continued, 'So how are you getting home? Do you need a lift?'

Hmmm, was soooo tempted, but I knew if I left my bike overnight, I'd have to brave the Hellbus to school in the morning.

Shudder.

'No thanks, Sir. I've got my bike outside.'

'Oh right, I didn't know you were a cyclist,' he said, looking pleased. 'I'm a proper bike nut myself. Good for you. OK, as long as you make sure you put your lights on. And thanks again for all your help. I couldn't have wished for a better assistant – you're a star!'

And then HE PUT HIS ARM ROUND ME! Only a quick squeeze and a smile, but my knees went from liquefied to entirely absent.

Brilliant first auditions, smooth as clockwork.

Happy happy happy me!

Mr J thinks I am a 'star'!

And he HUGGED ME.

APRIL 3RD

I pedalled like an Olympic gold medallist to get to school by quarter to eight this morning, ready to iron out the details on the second lot of auditions tonight. Quickly nipped to the loos to check I wasn't too helmet-headed before going to our form room. Mr J was already sitting behind his desk, head in his hands, shirt crumpled and hedgehog-hair spiking up. It took Jedi Master self-control not to reach out and smooth it down. He looked so scruffy and so cute.

'Morning, Sir.'

'Oh, hello, Lara, come in,' he said. 'The buses can't be in yet surely.'

'Came on my bike, Sir. I wanted to show you the draft poster for the final so you can see if there's anything that needs changing. If you like it, I could see the marketing lady today. I've spoken to her already and she said she just needs a couple of days to get them printed up. The tickets are already done and . . .'

He didn't seem to be paying any attention. 'Sir?'

'Oh, sorry.' Sitting up, he shook his head slightly. 'Tickets, yes, that's great. Let's have a look at this poster then.'

Any spare time I've had this week has been devoted

to getting it perfect. The pen-and-ink illustrations in the background stand out against the pinky violet colourwash and the collage made from the audition and rehearsal shots creates a 3D contrast. It took me HOURS. And Mr J's reaction made it worth every single second.

He drew the poster carefully out of the folder, studying the detail without speaking. Eventually he looked up at me. 'This is amazing. My goodness, is there anything you can't do?'

The glow spread through my whole body. 'I'm glad you like it, Sir.'

'Like it?' he said. 'It's absolutely fantastic! It's hard to believe someone your age could do this.'

I beamed. 'I promise it's all my work. It took me forever.'

'Wow,' he said, staring down at the poster again. 'I am blown away by your talent, Lara. And for all the help you've given me with the show. Thank you.'

'Oh, Sir, thank *you*. I'm loving doing it,' I said.

Loving being with you, Mr J.

For the rest of the day, I was walking on sunshine. Which is v. unusual for me as my default state is trudging through a concrete swamp in two-ton boots.

The auditions went without a hitch again, but the acts weren't as good as yesterday's. 'Magic Mark' was first with some OK-ish card tricks, but he was shaking so much he dropped the whole deck at one point. Pity. Then dancing twins, 'Seeing Double', from Year 7, who had a punch-up onstage and had to be separated by Mr J. (Riotous applause for that.)

Finally we had the talent-free Miss Molly Horridly-Jones, slaughtering Adele's 'Someone Like You' badly enough to make me want to claw my ears off.

Unfortunately, as we'd scraped right through the barrel tonight, I had to agree with Mr J to put Molly through.

Grrr.

He rolled his eyes at me while she was singing! (Still tinged with red, but if anything, even more gorgeous.) That proves we think the same: there's no need for words on our shared wavelength. And he seems to be the only other person who sees through Molly's 'nice girl' act for the adults. Even Mum's fallen for it.

God, I wish I had another picture of him as well as the Facebook screensaver one. Maybe one that looks more like he does now. I was wondering how to sneak a snap with my phone today, but if he caught me doing it, I would literally *die* of mortification.

He didn't offer me a lift again tonight, but I've started thinking maybe even the Hellbus would be tolerable if the pay-off was an extra half an hour on my own with him.

Oh, Mr J. My life would be a desert of complete unbearability without you as my metaphorical oasis/ watering hole. You are the only person on earth (apart from Emma, and possibly Gran) who actually seems to enjoy my company. No one else even likes me, not my so-called former friends and apparently not even my own family.

Yet ANOTHER row tonight with Dad over some minor misdemeanour. Can't even remember what triggered it off, it was that insignificant. I tuned out early, but the odd phrase filtered through '. . . behave like a delinquent . . . done to deserve this . . . worked all the hours God sent . . . get a minute's peace in my own home.'

V. apparent he has absolutely no idea what most kids my age get up to if he thinks I, the Mother Teresa of Teenagers, am out of control. Maybe I should go on a shoplifting spree. Post some saucy selfies. Date a guy with prison tats and a dog called Tyson.

Yeah, that'll teach him.

Mum, Dad, this is Keith.

Nice to meet you. Call me Psycho, all my friends do.

APRIL 5TH

That bitch.

I swear I'm going to KILL Molly.

Sitting on my bed writing this entirely BOILING with rage. I have never been so embarrassed in my life. Even tops the horror of Bogphoto.

That evil BITCH.

At break, everything was great. Me and Mr J were chatting about the show and life stuff in the classroom when there was a knock at the door.

'Is it OK to come in, Sir?' said Molly, trailed by Mikaela and Chloe.

'Of course,' he said, smiling at them in an ordinary *I'm-your-teacher-so-this-is-what-I-have-to-do* way, not the genuine *I-like-you-as-a-person* kind he saves for me. Molly's expression was studiedly serious, but I noticed she still worked the tits and teeth for all they were worth. Slapper.

'Sir, it's quite a delicate subject . . .' She glanced over at me then back to him.

'Could you wait outside, Lara, please?' he said.

I decided to make the most of this rare opportunity to visit the toilets without fear. When I returned, the three witches were leaving, each smirking as she passed me; smirks which exploded into shrieks of laughter as they disappeared outside.

I can hardly face writing what happened next. Total humiliation. I mean it, I am going to kill that bitch if it's the last thing I ever do.

The Most Embarrassing Conversation of My Life

Mr Jagger: Right. OK. I need to have a word with you about something. It's a bit difficult though.

Me: What is it, Sir?

Mr Jagger: Well, it's just that Molly has refused to use the changing rooms for the final if you're going to be in there.

Me: Why?

Mr Jagger: Now, I don't want you thinking for a minute I believe this, but she said you've got lice.

Me: ?

Mr Jagger: I said it was ludicrous.

Me: (raging on the inside) I haven't got lice, Sir. Or anything like that. She's having you on.

Mr Jagger: (visibly relieved) Well, you know if you needed to, we could always arrange for the school nurse to —

Me: I don't have lice. I don't need the nurse.

Mr Jagger: Good, I'll have a word with Molly. She really is childish.

Me: No! I mean, no it's fine, just a joke. Honestly, I'm not bothered. Can we get on with the scheduling, please?

I don't know how I'm going to do it, but I am going to get you back for this one day. Molly Hardy-Jones, you are *dead*.

APRIL 6TH

First thing this morning, I took the Cambridge consent form over to the boys' school. I've been over twice now and both times the secretary's fobbed me off, saying she's too busy. (Finally) handed them to Miss Longbottom, as instructed by Mr J. Boy oh boy, do her people skills need some work.

Me: Hello, Mr Jagger told me to give this to you.

Grumpy Cow Secretary: (snatching) Did he now. What is it?

Me: Oh. Er, it's the permission slip for the Cambridge trip.

GCS: Where's your cheque?

Me: What cheque?

GCS: (tutting) The cheque for the transport.

Me: Oh, Mr Jagger said he'd sort that out. He said school would pay my expenses.

GCS: Why?

Me: Why what?

GCS: Why would he say that?

Me: Er, I don't know? Maybe you should speak to him.

GCS: Ha!

Me: Thanks, bye.

GCS: (grunt) And shut the door.

Me: (under breath) Grumpy cow.

GCS: What did you say?

Me: (running) Nothing!

Unbelievably moody mare.

Went to the form room at lunchtime to tell him I'd done it, but when I got there, he was on the phone, so I hovered around in the corridor. Obviously, I didn't *intend* to listen in, but the door was open so I couldn't help but overhear.

'No! I'm not going to change my mind. Please try to understand that.'

The floor creaked, making him look up. I mouthed, 'Sorry!' and started to back out, but he held a finger up, signalling me to wait. 'Look, I've got to go. I'll call you later . . . No, I don't know *when*, Dawn. After work sometime.'

'Sorry,' I said when he'd clicked it off, 'I didn't realise you were on the phone.'

He raked his fingers through his hair and my heart melted. Stress was creasing his lovely face and he looked sad and tired again, not his normal self at all.

'Hey, don't worry about it. You know my door is always open.'

'Except when it's shut, ha ha!' I said because I'm a twat who says twattish things when I'm nervous.

He nodded. 'But I would never shut my door to *you*, Lara. How can I help?'

My heart was saying, *Mr Jagger, you are the only decent thing in my life. I can't stop thinking about you. If I didn't have you, I'd probably kill myself.*

But luckily my mouth went, 'Er, I was wondering if

I could help *you*. You know, if you've got any jobs you want doing.'

'Not at the moment, thanks. Are you OK? Is there something bothering you?'

My golden ticket opportunity to get my own back on Molly.

His gorgeous face was full of genuine concern and, for a split second, I came so close to blurting out all about the bullying, my iPod, the bus, Sam, Chloe's defection, Bogphoto – the whole catalogue of gloom. I opened my mouth, then reality clobbered me: while my mum works for Molly's parents, I've got no choice but to put up and shut up.

Instead: 'I've handed in the permission slip for the Cambridge trip.'

'Great. Did you explain about the funding?'

'I tried to, but the secretary was a bit of a Rottweiler.' No response, so I gabbled on. 'Yeah, so she snatched the form off me and was really rude when I said you were sorting the money out. There should be a warning sign or something, you know – "dangerous dog".'

His smile had faded. 'Well, at least you got it done. Now sorry, but is there anything else? I need to get on with some work.'

'Er, n-no, nothing else, Sir. See you at the elimination tonight?'

He didn't even look up from his desk. 'Yes, see you there.'

And with that I left to skulk in the library, wondering, *What did I say to piss him off?!*

I spent all afternoon tied up in knots and by the time we got to the after-school performance I was on the edge of tears. To really brighten my mood (not), Mrs Muirhouse was there, making her first appearance as a guest judge. Although 'using the contestants' fragile egos as a whetstone for her tongue' might be a more accurate description for what went on. Ouch.

'I think you may be in the wrong place, dear. This is a *talent* show. Talll-ennntttt.'

Poor Reanne! Fair enough, she sings like a donkey with terminal tonsillitis, but still . . . Mrs Muirhouse, you are too cruel for school.

Second on stage was little Danny Hudson from Year 7. I cringed watching him mount the steps. How would he cope with the tongue o' nine tails flaying his self-esteem? But he got a well-deserved standing ovation and even Mrs Muirhouse said his guitar playing 'showed promise'. So he'll definitely be up for a Brit Award in the next few years.

The final act, however, was a massacre: three Year 8 girls singing out-of-tune harmonies.

'Maybe on your own YOU might have a chance,' said Mrs Muirhouse, pointing as they huddled nervously on the stage. 'Not you two, that one there. Yes, you. The one who looks like a meerkat. You sound passable. The other two though: you put the cack in cacophony. Absolutely dreadf—'

'Thaaaaank you, Mrs Muirhouse!' interrupted Mr Jagger, suddenly clapping very loudly. 'Great stuff, girls, well done, thank you so much. We're in a hurry tonight, so can we make sure we leave quickly, please? All the finalists will be announced next week. Thanks for coming, folks.'

Mr J left the hall as soon as the caretaker arrived to lock up, with just a casual 'Bye' tossed in my direction. My heart was a rock in my chest and my eyes were filling up as I traipsed out to the bike shed on autopilot.

What have I done? Why won't he talk to me?

I was unchaining my bike when I heard his voice, angrier than I'd ever heard it, almost shouting. I peeped out and there he was with a woman, both of them standing by his car. It was too gloomy to make out their faces, but then she moved, triggering the security light: Grumpy Cow Secretary!

In the shadows of the bike shed, I was invisible and I had a grandstand view of the pair of them. She grabbed his hand, but he pulled away, properly shouting.

'It won't make any difference whatever it is you've got to say.'

I couldn't make out her reply.

'Dawn, it is OVER.' He got in the car. 'I want my house keys back. *Please.*'

He raced out of the car park, tyres screeching at the exit. She just stood there while I watched her from the shadows, staring after him as he disappeared into the traffic. When she finally left, I snuck out with my bike and cycled home.

So it wasn't me he was angry with after all! I was in hell all day for no reason. And I cannot believe he ever went out with that miserable, slapped-arse-face cow! Honestly, you could not imagine two people less suited than Ms Grumpy Cow Secretary and Mr Perfect Jagger. They go together like leeches and cream.

Interestingly though, this does mean he's single. Not that I think for a minute he'd fancy a bit of Princess Gingernut here, because, duh, he's a teacher. But at least it means he can set about finding someone who deserves and appreciates him in a way that *she* clearly didn't. He's totally wasted on her. Actually, I bet he didn't even like her that much. And on that happy note I'll say *sweet dreams*.

Later . . . Mum and Dad have been arguing AGAIN; not even bothering to keep their voices down this time.

Simon ran in here, clutching his teddy, crying his eyes out, and stuck his head under the pillow. I didn't have the heart to kick him out, even though he snotted all over my clean duvet. I lay down and cuddled him, making up daft stories till he fell asleep. Then I carried him back to his own room and tucked him in with a kiss.

Mum and Dad were at it the whole time and they're STILL at it now. I wish I had my iPod.

Forgot to say, Chloe has unfriended me on Facebook so I guess that's the end of that then.

Her loss.

APRIL 9TH

I left home.

Only for one day, mind, and it wasn't exactly planned. I'm back now; for the time being at least. It was that disgusting, alcoholic pig's fault. I hate him, I absolutely HATE him.

It kicked off when instead of sulking in the loft with his pathetic trains as usual, he decided to bring his bad mood downstairs to the lounge. Me, Mum and Simon were watching telly, laughing and talking. Having a nice time for once. OK, so we'd turned the sound up a tiny bit to drown out the neighbours' heavy metal crap, but it wasn't loud. Dad, however, thought differently.

'Do you have to make that bloody racket?' he growled. 'Between Themnextdoor and you lot, I can't hear myself think.'

He crossed the room and thumped so hard on the wall that mine and Simon's school photos rattled. A second later and Themnextdoor upped the volume on 'Satan, Satan, Eat My Babies' even higher.

'Jesus Christ!' Dad yelled, hammering both fists on the wall.

'Give it a rest, Tony,' hissed Mum. 'You're just making it worse.'

Dad flipped. 'Don't you DARE tell me to give it a rest. I never get any peace from *your* nagging and now those bastards are making so much noise I can't even think straight.'

He crumpled up his beer can and threw it, missing the bin completely.

Pointedly looking at the can, Mum said, 'I don't think it's the noise that's affecting your ability to think, Tony.'

She turned to us two, sitting paralysed on the sofa. 'Go to your rooms, please, kids.'

'Aw, Mum –' started Simon.

'Now.'

Dad moved aside without a word and we both headed upstairs. Simon came in with me and put his hands over his ears and began to cry, very quietly, as I held him. Poor kid. I mean, *I* get scared so it must be miles worse for him; he was trembling and snuffling in my arms. I know he drives me crackers 99.9% of the time, but I can't stand seeing him in a state.

The muffled shouts grew louder, but the words still weren't clear because of Satan's little headbangers next door. I could pretty much guess what they were saying anyway; I've heard it enough times: *Money / drink / family / school fees / work, etc. etc.*

Then there was a pause followed by . . .

CRASH!

Next thing, Dad came pounding up the stairs and past my bedroom door. The loft ladder creaked under his weight as he went back up to the trains and I swear I could hear the *snap* of another ring pull. Putting my finger on my lips, I gestured at the door and Simon, wet-faced and hiccupy, nodded and stayed on the bed, hugging his teddy tight. I gave him a quick kiss and snuck off down the stairs.

Mum was in the lounge, sweeping up the remains of the big glass toucan, the one that's sat on the mantelpiece of every house we've ever lived in. Mum loves – *loved* – that bird because Dad bought it on their first wedding anniversary. He said it was a 'toucan of his love'. Cringe central, but soppy-cute and sweet. Well, Mum thought so. Now it lay smashed to pieces in the dustpan.

'Mum . . .' I said.

She looked up. 'Your dad didn't mean it, love. He's not himself at the moment.'

'I don't care. He's being horrible and it's scaring Simon. Why don't you tell him to stop?'

'Can't you see I'm trying? But he won't listen to a word I say any more.' She gestured at the broken glass. 'I'm tired of arguing with him. Half the time he just hides in the loft and, when I can get him to speak, he just wants a row.'

'What about Uncle Andy? He might listen to him.'

'Come here.' She folded me into a hug. 'Your Uncle Andy knows what's going on, love. And I have tried to get your dad to speak to him, but you know what he's like, he just clams up.'

Then she went on about how he's not very good at talking when things go wrong, how he blames himself for EVERYTHING: all the stuff with the business, money, having to move, Themnextdoor, Mum going out cleaning, struggling to pay for school, everyone being unhappy.

'I know he's behaving like a prize pillock at the moment. Believe me, I can't stand it when he's like this. But me, you and Simon are the most important things in his life. And he's got feeling guilty so mixed up with being angry at himself that he doesn't know how to deal with it.' She kissed the top of my head. 'Now, go upstairs and get ready for bed. I'll be up in a minute. I'm just going next door to try and reason with them.'

Whatever she said to them seemed to work (assuming it involved the word 'police') because they turned the sound right down. After she'd tucked Simon in, she came in to say goodnight, and even though she was sad and weary, it was good to feel like we were on the same side for once. And she did help me to see things a bit more from Dad's point of view, which made me feel sorry for him more than angry. For a while anyway.

I read my book for a bit and eventually drifted off to the sound of Dad's footsteps pacing above me in the loft.

That's when things got really weird.

I don't know how long it was before I woke up, but I know *what* woke me up: the sensation of a heavy, clammy body pushing me up against the wall. I sat bolt upright. Then I shoved, pushed, clambered over the person in my bed.

Dad.

The sick, sweet reek of lager coming off him was so revolting it made me gag. I crept in to Mum and shook her awake.

'Mum. Mum! Come quick.'

'Whaa . . . what is it, Lara? What's wrong?'

'Dad got into my bed and he's gone to sleep.'

She flung the covers back.

'He's really drunk. I don't know if he'll wake up.'

'Oh, he bloody well will, don't you worry,' she snapped, wide awake herself now. She marched straight into my bedroom, kicked aside Dad's discarded clothes then flooded the room with light. 'Tony!' Right in his ear. 'TONY! GET UP.'

Dad, drunk pig, snorted and turned over. Mum picked up an almost full glass of water from my bedside table and splashed the lot in his face. That worked.

'Whaaa!' he spluttered.

'Out. Now.' She dragged him up by the arm like a naughty kid and he lumbered to his feet, only his boxers on, staggering as she propelled him towards their room.

'Get back into bed now, Lara,' said Mum over her shoulder. 'We'll sort this out in the morning.'

But I couldn't. The pillow was sopping and the whole bed smelled rank so I went in with Simon instead. He didn't stir, but I hardly slept a wink. When it got light, I packed my rucksack with a few clothes and left a note.

Mum,
I am going to stay at Gran's.
Lara.

I didn't ring Gran to ask if it was OK, just let myself in after school. Tucked up under her ancient crocheted blanket, she seemed quite alert.

'Hello, Lara love. Your mum phoned me this morning to say you might be staying. I've made up the couch.'

'Thanks, Gran,' I said.

'Do you want to talk about it?'

'Not really.'

'Least said, soonest mended, eh? Good, I want to catch the rest of *Deal or No Deal*. Now, just pass me that bottle off the sideboard, will you? Are you hungry?'

'A bit,' I said.

'There's a Fray Bentos on the worktop,' she said, turning the telly to ear-splitting and wriggling deep into the chair. 'Help yourself.'

If you're seeking wise old Yoda-type advice, my gran is not the answer. I only stayed one night in the end; the springs in that sofa poke like rusty twigs. Plus it smells of wee.

Haven't spoken to Dad since I got home. He's been hiding out up in the loft and I've been hiding in my room. My mind is totally scrambled.

Why can't he just go back to being normal Dad? I hate him, then I feel bad for hating him because it's my fault he's in this mess and it keeps going round and round in my head. I think about him stinking out my bed, too drunk to find his way to his own room.

Disgusting.

But then I remember, if it wasn't for my school fees, he wouldn't be stressed and drink in the first place.

God, I am so confused. And I didn't even get to see Mr Jagger today because he was out on another pointless training course. Not one teeny-tiny solitary good thing has happened in my whole day.

APRIL 10TH

When I got back from my evening round, Mum and Dad were waiting in the lounge with their We've Got Some Bad News faces on.

'What is it? What's up?' I said to Mum, panicking. 'Is it Gran? Has something happened?'

'No, it's not your gran. It's me and your dad.' She glanced at Dad before she continued. 'There's no easy way to say this, love: we've decided to have a trial separation.'

'A *what*?'

'A trial separation. Your dad's going to move out for a while to give us both a bit of space to –'

'What your mother means,' interrupted Dad, grinding his fag into the ashtray, 'is that now I've lost the fancy job and the fancy house, she doesn't fancy *me* any more. So she's kicking me out.'

'Tony, that is not true and you know it,' said Mum.

'Lara, I – we – need you to understand that things have been very difficult for your father and me recently, what with losing the house and the business. You know the stress we've been under.'

Dad breathed out heavily through his nose.

'It's been a tough couple of years and now we need some time apart to consider our options for the future,' she continued, ignoring him.

'But it's only temporary, right?' I said. Dad watched Mum, but didn't speak.

'I will always love your dad,' Mum said carefully, 'but I can't live with him. Not the way things are at the mo–'

'The way things are?' Dad exploded. 'And that's all my fault too, I suppose, eh, Jo? I *asked* to go bust? I *chose* to move to this shithole? It was *my* decision to turn down the job with Andy and sit on my backside all day?'

'Tony, we agreed, remember? Not in front of the kids.'

Dad drew in his breath like he was about to say something, then sighed instead and headed out of the room. At the last minute he wheeled back round.

'I'm taking the dog. Don't even try to stop me.'

When he'd gone, Mum said, 'Please don't mention this to Simon yet. It's best if I do it. He'll only get upset.'

Be the one to tell Simon his parents are splitting up?

No worries on that score, Mum. I'd rather dance the tonsil tango with Sam Short.

Oh God, I suppose it was inevitable, given the awfulness of things recently. And I know I hate him and he's been a nightmare to live with lately.

But I never wanted this to happen.

APRIL 11TH

Only a week to go till my birthday. That means only seven more days until I can:

- Move out of the family home.
- Get married.
- Have sex.
- And (according to the Gospel of Wikipedia) sell scrap metal. (Er, fab.)

When I got in from school (post blessedly uneventful day) I tripped over one of the boxes of junk lining the hall. 'Your dad's coming back for those later,' Mum said, wandering out of the kitchen dressed in yesterday's leggings and a scruffy T-shirt. The house smelled different. Cleaner.

'The dog's gone then?'

She nodded. Simon's face was blotchy and he had his arms wrapped round Mum's legs so tight he didn't even notice she was dropping fag ash on his head.

Poor kid, he's been devastated since she told him. Of course it's horrible for me and Mum too, but he's only little. I need to start being much, much nicer to him. From this day forth: no more hanging him on coat hooks by his jumper; no more verbal abuse and DEFINITELY no more violence of any description. I shall become full of older sisterly tolerance and niceness. I will never smack him again.

Unless he *really* asks for it.

'Don't say anything to your gran either,' Mum warned. 'Your dad wants to talk to her first.'

Dropped in to see her after my paper round. She was in another rare lucid (i.e. near-sober) mood so we had a cup of tea together and a chat. She must know something's up at home. Not as daft as she makes out, is Gran.

'It's your birthday soon, isn't it?' she said. 'Anything you'd like in particular?'

Long shot, I know, but I have wanted one of these for so long now and I just daren't ask Mum and Dad for anything at the moment.

'I really, really want a Kindle, Grandma.'

'What's that?'

'A Kindle.'

'A what?'

'A KINDLE.'

She nodded. 'Right, love. Well, I'll see what I can do. Friday, is it?'

'Yes,' I answered. 'A week today.'

Oooo, a Kindle! How fabulous would that be? Fifteen years of china kittens and hot-water bottle covers and finally she's going to get me something I'll actually use.

A Kindle!

That would just be the dog's dangles. Mr J loves his; he's always going on about it. Loads of the books he said I should read are out of copyright and that means they'll be dead cheap on there. And my room is so tiny, I'm in imminent danger of being entombed in a book avalanche so a Kindle could quite possible save my life.

And, as it seems highly unlikely I'll be moving out *or* having sex *or* getting married *or* selling scrap metal on the big day, at least getting a Kindle will give me something to celebrate.

Further gadget goodness: according to my calculations, I should have enough saved for a replacement iPod by the end of next month.

Yay!

Later . . . Had to sneak the light on so I don't wake Simon. He crept into bed with me earlier looking so sad and tiny, like a baby bird fallen out of its nest. I feel dead sorry for him. He doesn't get what's happening. Whereas I am still spitting feathers over the Bed Incident, he's just gutted Dad's gone. It's heartbreaking listening to him crying into his teddy.

And also, why did I never realise what a little fiery furnace he is? This is the warmest I've been in ages.

Toasty!

APRIL 12TH

Because the atmosphere at home was so hideous, what with Mum's misery and Simon's wailing, I buggered off to the library, armed with the list of books from Mr Jagger. I was chaining the bike up when I heard someone calling my name.

Speak of the devil!

'Lara!' He jogged right up to me. 'I thought it was you. Enjoying your weekend?'

I might have managed a 'hollow laugh' had I not been so blisteringly self-conscious of my skanktastic jeans and sweatshirt combo. Cheeks a brighter shade of beetroot from the ride; sweaty helmet-hair plastered to my head.

Marvellous.

He, naturally, looked immaculate, maybe on his way back from a modelling shoot for Abercrombie & Fitch.

'Yes, thanks. See you on Monday!' I said. In my desperation to stop him getting a good look at me, I tripped on the stone steps.

Shame squared. Mortification cubed. Humiliated to infinity and beyond.

He immediately knelt down where I was sprawled, reaching a hand out. 'God, Lara, are you OK?'

'I think so, Sir,' I said, hobbling to my feet. Wasn't OK though. It absolutely *killed* my knees; they're black and blue.

'That looks really painful. You should probably sit down for a minute. Tell you what, let me buy you a coffee.'

He looked up and down the street. 'Look, there's a Costa. Can you limp that far?'

Him: vision of perfection. Me: sweaty tramp.

NOOOOO!

'Honestly, I'm fine. I'd better go.' I gritted my teeth and smiled.

Now of course am thinking, *Was that the right thing to do?*

An alternate reality is plaguing me in which I have *not* just shattered both kneecaps; I am *not* wearing a 'Take That Reunion Tour' sweatshirt and I am *not* sweating like a pig at a barbecue. Groomed and glam in my Ted Baker dress and shoes, he takes my hand and we skip off for a romantic choca-mocha-ccino *à deux*.

But then I'm back in the land of *Life Sucks When You're Lara T.*

'Well, if you're sure,' he said, and with that, the chance had gone.

Nothing, I repeat *nothing*, good to report about the rest of this weekend. Dad came for the remaining boxes and, after he left, I found a miniature signalman poking out from under the doormat. That must mean he doesn't see it as temporary. I mean, there isn't even enough space for him to set the trains up in his quote grotty bedsit unquote.

That's when it hit me like a meteorite: my parents are splitting up.

THIS IS REAL.

Simon was howling, pleading with Dad to stay. He velcroed himself round his leg like a runny-nosed koala. Not the most dignified of exits.

I stayed at the top of the stairs as am still feeling weird near him. Dad paused, framed in the doorway, his arms full of junk. All choked up, he turned. 'For better and for worse, eh, Jo?'

Mum stood there, a red-eyed zombie. 'Just go, Tony, please.'

Themnextdoor slow handclapped over the fence as Dad loaded the boot. I can't bring myself to write Dad's response down here. Suffice it to say there were several words Simon was unfamiliar with. Mum went all tight-lipped and ordered him inside.

When Dad had driven off, she wrapped her arms round Simon while they both sobbed and sobbed, which was absolutely soul-destroying. I haven't seen Mum cry like that since she accidentally scratched the dining-room table.

Emma already knew about Dad moving out as apparently he spoke to Uncle Andy yesterday. I rang her tonight for a moan.

'My dad told him to come and stay here for a few

weeks,' she told me, 'but he said he'd miss you and Simon too much.'

Ha! Sure he would. He was only interested in Paddington when he left, who has had to come back as there's a pet ban in the flats. Beyoncé, beside himself with joy, has spent all day howling. Mum now at the end of her tether.

'Dad's dead worried about him, you know. He said he sounded really depressed, keeps saying he can't live without your mum.'

Melodramatic as it sounds, I do actually believe it. If it was anyone else, I'd say that is bollocks, but Mum and Dad are – were – the happiest couple you could ever meet. Well, until the business went belly up. Up till then, they were well loved-up; they used to hold hands when they went out, even if it was just to the shops.

They haven't done that for months. (Held hands OR been out together.)

Anyway, we're supposed to be seeing Dad on Tuesday because he's taking us to McDonald's in town for our tea. I'm not really sure I want to see him (or have my tea at McDonald's) because I can't stop being angry and embarrassed about the Bed Incident.

I *get* he's in a bad way and I *know* he's got a lot of

worries and everything, BUT getting so drunk you mistakenly get into bed with your own daughter? Ugh, revolting beyond words. It creeps me out just to be near him, like he's not even my dad any more.

How Things Stand Now
- Mum and Dad are splitting up.
- Dad's a disgusting drunken pig.
- Mr J invites me for a drink (sort of) and I have to turn it down.

So at least it won't matter much if I fail all my GCSEs. I've already got a PhD in Being Crap.

APRIL 13TH
All quiet on the bitches front so looks like the avoidance plan is holding up (touch wood) with the bonus side effect of mucho quality time with Mr Jagger at breaks, working on prep for the show. He was telling me all sorts about when he was at uni today. Stuff like where he lived, the 'high jinks' with his friends, the boring Mcjobs he had in the holidays.

No mention of Grumpy Cow Secretary though, so

still haven't got a clue how long they were together for. Maybe he was with her at uni. I was dying to ask but it's not the sort of thing you can say to a teacher, is it?

Why on earth did you go out with Dawn of the Dead, Sir?

He's so inspirational, done so much, travelled to loads of different places. After college, he worked on a soccer camp in America and that's what made him decide to be a teacher. Then he volunteered at a school in Tanzania for three months and he's planning on going back in the summer holidays to help them build a new classroom. He's such a kind guy.

Inevitably, I got the jealous evils from the Three Fuckwiteers in English, but so what? Mr Jagger likes me! All the girls fancy him, but it's ME, Lara T, he wants to share his life story with. *I'm* the one he asked to help him with the show. *I'm* the one he picked to go on the Cambridge trip.

Give up thrusting your cleavage at him, Molly, you sad slapper. Men like Mr J are interested in the contents of a girl's mind, not her bra. And you might have a rack the size of Wembley, but the contents of your head wouldn't fill a *matchbox*.

Get it? Jog on, Molly. He's not interested.

Anyway, while we were talking, he told me more

about the Cambridge trip. He's been drafting the itinerary and he said it won't all be lectures. We'll have a tour of the city and 'experience student life' as well.

I. Cannot. Wait!

Although right now I'd be happy to have a tour of a skip and experience hobo life if it meant I didn't have to be at home. Can't face seeing Simon so quiet and low. And Mum is virtually catatonic, always either out working, staring into space or smoking.

When I got in tonight, she was curled up on the sofa, leafing through her wedding album. 'Hello, love. How was school?'

Same old, same old, Mum. I have no friends, most of the teachers ignore me. But hey ho, at least no one took a photo of me on the bog.

'Yeah, fine. How was your day?'

'Oh, you know, nothing special,' she said. 'I have got something that might cheer you up though. I saw Molly when I was just leaving the Hardy-Joneses. She said to tell you she's got a surprise for your birthday. Isn't that nice?'

WTF?!

Mum was packing the album in tissue paper so she didn't see my expression.

Putting on my best nonchalant voice, I went, 'Oh right, did she say what it is?'

Mum carefully lowered the album back into its box. 'No, but she did say you won't be expecting it. Oh, and she asked if she could friend you on Facebook or if you had Twitter or Insta-whatsit. I told her I'm sure you'd be thrilled.'

#OverMyDeadBody

'Er, great.'

Molly hates my guts in the real world so there's only one reason she'd be my friend in the virtual one. God, the thought she could keep tabs outside school too – yikes. It'd be like having her beady eyes mounted on my bedroom wall, following my every move.

Brain flinch. Have maxed up all my privacy settings just in case she tries.

'Have you spoken to your dad today?'

'He sent me a text saying meet him straight from school tomorrow in town. Me and Simon. That OK?'

'Yeah, course. Did he say anything else?'

He hadn't. I could tell Mum wanted me to say he said he missed us, but I don't think that's Dad's style nowadays. Since he lost the business, he's been turning into someone I don't even recognise any more. Mum too.

The smoking, for example. Neither of them used to smoke. Well, when they first met, but not for years and years. They've both started up again because we're multi-millionaires. Oh, hang on, we're not, are we? Yep, makes perfect sense. They used to go mental when people smoked within two metres of us. Now they don't think twice about puffing over us day and night like a pair of industrial furnaces. We *stink*. It's in our clothes, books, hair. Gross.

But it's not just the fags; there are loads of worse things too. Like we used to hug each other, eat together, talk, before we became these people who co-exist in the same space, not strangers exactly, but nowhere near a family. Lodgers who feel comfortable acting mean to each other maybe.

If we'd moved to Little Dunmow when Uncle Andy & Co did, I guarantee we'd be a million per cent happier. I'd still have Em, I could be enjoying school (or at least not hating it, hopefully) and, the biggie, Dad would have a good job on a plate. But of course, that's another SACRIFICE they made for my education. So what does that mean?

Yep, *everyone's* a loser and it's all because of ME.

Anyway, need to get on with my homework now.

English AND geography essays to do tonight. They're really piling it on at the moment; not long till the exams start. Year 11 seems to be flying past. At least that's one thing in my control: if I get decent grades, maybe it'll make the SACRIFICES seem more worthwhile.

After that, I've still got some last-minute wrinkles to iron out in the grand finale itinerary for Friday. Now the auditions are over and the acts are sorted, just need to check the running order works and all the tickets have been collected. Setting the alarm extra early tomorrow so I can get the papers finished pronto and be in the classroom when Mr J arrives.

I love love LOVE that bit of the day when it's just us talking and there's no one else around to interrupt/ stare/laugh/make stupid, snidey comments, etc. I feel like I've known him forever. No one will ever understand me the way he does.

Maybe that's why, deep down, I'm actually glad we didn't move away because if we had, I would never have met Mr J.

He thinks I'm beautiful!!!!

I got in before he did this morning and was already engrossed in the master timetable when he arrived.

'Perfect,' he said, pulling the chair up next to me. 'You've thought of everything. You have rescued me from organising a shambles.'

'No, Sir, you've done a great job,' I protested.

'Well, it's nice you've got such confidence. But seriously, you've been fantastic. I am so impressed: organising the acts, the sets, the publicity virtually by yourself. All I have to do is turn up and waffle a bit onstage. You don't need me at all.'

Oh, Mr Jagger, you have no idea!

Then he said this: 'Brains and beauty. You're a lucky girl.'

I went instantly red, muttered, 'Thanks,' and didn't know what else to say. No one's ever called me beautiful before. (Except Mum and Dad. And Emma. But family doesn't count.)

Mr J thinks I'm beautiful!

Ha! Grumpy Cow Secretary must have finally got the message she was punching well above her (heavy) weight and backed off as he was definitely on tip-top form today. Relaxed and chatty. No tired eyes or stressy face. Good. He started raving about *Jane Eyre*: he'd brought his uni copy with all the notes in for me to borrow. But I was too caught up in being near him to concentrate properly.

It's a mystery why he's a teacher when he could have been an actor or a model or some megabucks job like that. But for me his looks aren't the main event; what makes him so special is he's the only person I've ever met (apart from Emma) who is totally tuned in to my wavelength. Therefore, even if his face moonlighted as Wayne Rooney's stunt-bum, I'd still think he was perfect.

When he leaned across me to point out a quote, I came over all 'loosen my corset strings and pass me the sal volatile'. This week I'm definitely off to Boots on Saturday to try every bottle of aftershave till I find out what he wears. The man smells as good as he looks. Quite something.

Mikaela was (unintentionally) funny in PSHE. We were doing some tedious pointlessness on the effects of smoking.

'Anyone?' asked Mr J.

'Makes you smell.' 'Lung cancer.' 'Wrecks your gums.'

'Excellent. Anything else? Anyone?'

'Sir?'

'Yes, Mikaela.'

'You know how it makes your fingers turn yellow . . .?'

'Yeees . . .'

'Well, does it make your toes turn yellow too?'

I snorted softly, even though I knew I'd pay for it later, but bollocks, I couldn't help it. Mikaela is so dumb, her brain couldn't find the right answer if you gave it a compass and a fifteen-minute head start.

After school in Maccy D's and Dad looked terrible, shredding paper napkins until the tabletop was like the bottom of a hamster's cage. Simon hardly said a word, just slurped his Coke through a straw, occasionally breaking off into operatic burping. Honestly, you cannot take him anywhere. But as I have vowed to be a saintly sister, I didn't smack him or drop ice cubes down his neck or anything.

Even so, we didn't have a good time. Dad barely spoke and all I wanted to say was, 'How could you do that to me?' because he's never even said sorry, but he looked so miserable, I left it.

I don't really hate him. I know I said I did, but I didn't

mean it. I *am* finding it hard to forgive him though. Not just for that night, but for being such a complete arse to me, Mum and Simon recently. And I'm embarrassed, I guess, and he must be too.

This love him/hate him thing is doing my head in. I mean, he's still my *dad*, but at the same time he's a stranger. It is so messed up.

When you're a kid, you think your parents are invincible, then one day you learn they're every bit as vulnerable as you are. Families are so fragile. Perhaps the moment you realise that is when you *really* grow up.

<u>McDonald's Conversation</u>

Dad: How's your Mum?

Me: Yeah, fine.

Simon: *Sluuuuurp.*

Dad: How's Paddington?

Me: Yeah, fine.

Simon: *Sluuuurp.*

Dad: You seen your gran?

Me: Yeah, she said she's getting me a Kindle for my birthday.

Dad: A Kindle? Crikey, that's generous. How's school?

Me: *Well, today I laughed at Mikaela in PSHE. So at*

lunchtime someone put a used Tampax in my sandwich box.
But I can live with that because MR JAGGER THINKS I'M
BEAUTIFUL! Yeah, fine.

Simon: *Buuuuurp.*

I have sussed the situation out and the situation is not
good. There's so much space between us all, I honestly
can't see how we could ever get close again. Maybe it's
time to face the fact that my family is permanently broken.

Later . . . Unknown Sender: *Hope you liked your little*
lunchtime treat. Sorry we didn't have time to wrap it up.

Sent one back: *Drop dead, Molly.*

Quelle surprise, no reply.

APRIL 17TH

5.40 a.m. and even though my alarm went off ten minutes
ago, I didn't need it. About half two, I sat bolt upright,
practically hyperventilating from this unbelievably vivid
nightmare about Dad having a psycho flip-out. I couldn't
have gone back to sleep if you'd paid me.

Assuming it's because I'd seen a news story about a
man going on a mad rampage after his business went tits

up. The experts were talking about the effects of money worries, marriage on the rocks, no way forward, etc. They said it's on the rise in the recession, a recognised act called 'family annihilation', so I searched it and Tony 'angry/moody/withdrawn/financial problems' Titliss doesn't just fit the profile, he IS the profile.

Had to ring him.

'Lara, do you know what time it is?' he said.

'Sorry, Dad. I just need to ask you something.'

'Me too, now I think on it. Next time, do you want to go for a pizza instead of McD?'

!!

'Dad, listen to me. You're not planning on doing anything stupid, are you?'

'What do you mean by "stupid"?'

'I know things are bad between you and Mum and you're worried about money, but things will get better. Honest.'

There was a long pause.

'Lara, shall I come round? We can talk about this properly.'

'No, Dad! Not while you're angry like this.'

He sounded shocked, 'I'm not angry, love. What's going on?'

'Nothing. Just checking. You know, better to be safe . . .'

'Where do you get this stuff from?'

'Forget it, Dad. It's OK. See you later. Bye.'

'La–'

So, fingers crossed, panicking for nothing.

Later . . . Bloody hell.

It's my sixteenth birthday *tomorrow*. The final of the show is *tomorrow*. I get to spend the whole afternoon and evening with Ben 'Perfect' Jagger *tomorrow*. The most important day of my entire life is *tomorrow*.

And I have a spot on my chin so big you could find it on Google Earth.

APRIL 18TH

My Sixteenth Birthday. The Talent Show Final.

Oh my God! I can hardly write this, my hands are shaking that much. Oh my God, oh my God! It's really late, nearly midnight in fact, on what has to be the weirdest (but best by MILES) day of my whole life so far. My birthday too! It's like something out of a film.

Oh my God, oh my God, oh my God. Did I *dream* tonight?

The final of We've Got Talent! with staff, parents (not mine though) and a massive crowd of kids from both schools packing out the hall. Molly got eliminated first. Ha!

Mrs Muirhouse's tongue was set to caustic: 'I don't mean to be rude, Molly, but there are countries in the world where you'd have been stoned to death for that performance. You sing about as well as my cat plays chess and, well, let's just say Mr Biscuits hasn't beaten me yet.'

Good golly, Miss Molly! I thought she was going to explode, but she had to pretend to laugh it off. *Sweet*.

Danny Hudson and his guitar came runner-up and Graham Flett won, singing 'Walking in the Air' from that cartoon at Christmas.

When I saw old Jabbamoobs done up as an April Santa, I thought that would be the most surreal experience of the day. But oh, how wrong I was. What came next made that seem positively mundane.

Avoided Molly-centric aggro all evening by sticking close to Mr Jagger. (Ben? I don't even know what to call him now.) She must have slipped out into the car park straight after Mrs M's verbal annihilation, but I didn't notice as was too caught up making sure the night ran like clockwork. (Which it did.) When Mr J called it a day after the awards ceremony, we packed up together, but there wasn't much to do so he let me go.

I was so mega-happy it'd been a success and if it was a bit deflating, knowing it was over, thinking about Cambridge kept me cheery. Anyway, that's not the important bit. It's what happened later that matters.

People went off home, I said goodbye and headed over to the bike rack, blissfully clueless that would be where Molly had left my Birthday Surprise.

My bike.

Both tyres slashed, chain ripped off and lights smashed in. My beautiful bike, the one I slaved over two paper rounds to buy, destroyed.

Well, Molly was right, it was *definitely* a surprise.

And to make things worse, it was nine o'clock at night and I was stuck at school; no money for a bus, no credit on my phone and suppose I had, what then? Mum couldn't leave Simon and I can't remember the last time Dad was under the limit after teatime. I didn't fancy a long dark walk home at this time of night either. So I did the only thing I could, given the circumstances: I sat on the ground and burst into tears.

Next thing, I heard a man's voice calling out. 'Hello? Everything all right in there?' Then Mr J peered into the bike shelter. 'Lara? Is that you?'

I sniffed, 'Yes, sir.' And tried to stop crying, but I couldn't. Molly's vandalism was the last straw and I was a gibbering, bawling, red-faced mess.

'Good God. What happened to your bike?' He wheeled it under the light.

(It was – is – completely wrecked by the way. Absolutely no idea how I'll afford a new one. Ebay a kidney?)

He took a packet of tissues out of his pocket and handed them to me. I blew my nose, breathing in gasps till I calmed down enough to speak.

'It's OK,' he said. 'I'll give you a lift home.'

'But it's too far, Sir!' I said. 'It doesn't matter, honestly, I can walk.'

'At this time of night? I don't think so,' he said, lifting the corpse of my bike into his boot. 'Come on. Get in.'

So I did.

His scruffy old car was crammed with work and sports gear. 'Excuse the mess,' he said, sweeping an armful of exercise books off the passenger seat. I carried on wiping my eyes with his tissue while surreptitiously checking my mascara hadn't run, praying I didn't look too much like a deranged panda.

When we were pulling out of the car park, he asked, 'Do you want to talk about it?' I shook my head. He was quiet for a minute before he tried again. 'Lara.' He tapped his fingers on the steering wheel. 'Tell me who did that to your bike. I want their names, please.'

'Dunno,' I said automatically, turning to stare out of the window. 'It's left at the lights.'

'Well, if you don't want to tell me, that's fine, but you are going to have to tell *someone*. I know you think you're being brave putting up with this, but it's ridiculous.'

'I don't know what you mean,' I said lamely.

'Oh, come on, for such an intelligent girl, you really are being daft. You don't need to put up with any of it. Go and see Mrs Ellis and tell her everything. In fact, I'm taking you to see her the first day after the holidays, straight after registration. No arguments.'

'No! You can't do that,' I said.

'But you're putting up with this unnecessarily.' I could hear the frustration in his voice. 'Molly is a jealous bully and, by the way, don't try to deny it, I do know it's her. She deserves to be punished for what she'd done and made to stop. And you, what must you think of yourself, letting her get away with it? Like I said, no arguments. You and I are going to see Mrs Ellis and we're going to tell her everything.'

Of course, I knew that must NEVER happen so I went all crazy, wailing madwoman. He pulled over at a bus stop and waited patiently till I stopped.

'I don't understand why you feel you can't confide in anyone. If not Mrs Ellis, why not me? I mean, I'm not hard to talk to, am I?'

I shook my head, took a deep breath and, gross though it sounds, it was like vomiting up my emotions. No way I could stop the words from spilling out once I'd started. How Molly and me were never Billy Best-mates, but it wasn't this bad before. Then about Mum and Dad losing the house and that stuff, Dad moving out; how hard things are financially and what the bike means to me.

And then that led on to the bullying. I didn't give him the darkest, deepest humiliating details though. Skimmed over the X-rated stuff. Tell him Sam tried to see my boobs on the bus? No chance. And I edited out the Molly/Mum work threats because Mum needs job-related hassles like a hole in the head, especially with Dad gone.

'So that's why I've decided I'm not coming back after the holidays,' I finished, making my hair fall like a curtain to hide my blotchy face. 'I can't take any more of this. And if Mum and Dad are disappointed, they'll just have to put up with it because I swear, I will kill myself before I go back. I had *two* paper rounds to buy that bike! And it's my *birthday* today!'

'Lara, look at me.'

I turned. The streetlight had given him a golden halo and his expression was so concerned and sincere it nearly set me off blubbing again.

'You are worth a thousand Mollys, Mikaelas and Chloes. You're an incredibly intelligent, talented, funny, beautiful girl; the kind of girl they dream of being and because they will, no matter how much money they've got, NEVER be like you, they're jealous.'

I almost laughed out loud. 'They're not *jealous* of me. I'm a freak.'

'How can you say that?' He looked genuinely surprised. 'You're gorgeous, witty, interesting, you wipe the floor with *me* intellectually . . . For what it's worth, I think you're amazing.'

Any other time, I'd have thought I'd died and gone to heaven hearing those words coming from anyone's lips, let alone his. But I was too emotionally fried to properly take in what he was saying.

'I know it doesn't feel like that now,' he continued, 'and I understand school is a nightmare because these girls are such a pack of bitches – but it won't always be like this.'

He tilted my chin up to make me look in his eyes. 'You are very special. Trust me.'

I looked up at him, his hand still on my face, and that's when the atmosphere shifted. The air was charged with static from an off-the-Richter-scale *frisson*. I was looking into his eyes, he was looking into mine and we were both motionless. I couldn't breathe. Without any involvement from my brain, my lips moved towards his and he leaned in towards me . . . and then on to the horn.

BEEEEEEP!

Loud as a siren.

He jerked his head back like he'd been electrocuted.

'I should get you home,' he said after a few seconds. I stared fixedly at the dashboard, arms rigid as the engine sputtered back to life and we drove on without another word. But the FRISSON was still in the car with us, like a third passenger.

When we pulled up outside my house, he didn't even look at me, just went, 'Thanks for your help tonight. And happy birthday.'

I nodded, barely squeaking out a 'thanks for the lift' in reply. As I watched his tail lights disappear round the corner, I remembered my mangled bike in the boot. I suppose he'll just take it to the tip.

Came straight upstairs when I got in. Need space to think. I'm knackered, but my brain is fizzing like a sherbet dip dab. What just happened?

And more to the point, what was about to happen?

APRIL 19TH

Lara Jagger.

Lara J.

I've bitten my nails so far down my fingertips are bleeding. Every minute feels like an hour. Every hour feels like a day. First day of the Easter holidays. Ten no-school days and I want over already.

L Jagger.

Mrs L Jagger.

Can't eat. Can't sleep. I keep pacing up and down my room. Up and down. Up and down. Flop on bed.

Look out of window.

Read a page. Throw book down.

Stare in mirror.

Flop on bed.

Pick up sketch pad. Throw it down.

Stare in mirror.

Flop on bed.

Repeat.

Mr and Mrs B Jagger.

Ben Jagger.

I love him so much every bit of me aches. He said things to me that no one else ever has. I'm beautiful and funny and clever. That was not a conversation between a pupil and a teacher, it was . . . Oh, please, please, please, please let me have him. My fantastic, amazing boyfriend-to-be: fit, sporty, intelligent, caring, funny. Mr Perfectly Right.

Mrs Ben Jagger.

Mrs Lara Jagger.

Right, it's a tricky situation, I realise that. He's older than me (not much) and he's my teacher (not for long). But I love him, I can't help it. And it's no silly crush, it's the real thing.

Capital L-O-V-E *Love*.

Sitting with him in the car, both of us looking into each other's eyes, it was like a fairy-tale 'suddenly know' moment. Stars aligning. Jigsaw pieces falling into place and all that soulmate jazz.

I might only be sixteen but Gran's always said I'm an old head on young shoulders and anyway, he's not *that* much older than me. Seven years is nothing. Dad's *ten* years older than Mum and no one ever bats an eyelid. And Mr J's only my teacher temporarily. Mum was only a year older than me when she got together with Dad, and he was her *boss*.

He told me I'm beautiful! He said I was 'amazing'. Special. Unique. Every single precious word he's ever said to me is printed on my heart.

God, I need to talk to someone soooo bad. Dying to tell Emma, but I mustn't. Suppose she tells Uncle Andy and Auntie Amanda? The most incredible thing in my whole life has happened and I can't share it with anyone, even her. Not yet anyway, not until I know what we're going to do.

Come ON, new term. (And when have I ever wanted to get back to school?!!)

APRIL 25TH

So I've been in Little Dunmow for a few days. Got back this morning. Didn't take you, dear diary, because although there's no way Emma would go nosing through my stuff, I couldn't run the risk of Auntie Amanda picking you up. Backfired stupendously of course as I've had five days of knicker-wetting angst picturing Mum digging you out from under the wardrobe. Not that she did.

Phew.

I've never had such a massive secret before and I was BURNING to blurt it out, but I can't. I mustn't. Imagine: 'I think my teacher likes me. I mean *really* likes me.' They wouldn't understand; they'd misinterpret it and twist it into something wrong.

Auntie Amanda kept calling me 'Dolly Daydream' and I caught Emma looking at me strangely a couple of times. She did ask me if everything was OK, but I told her I was worried about Mum and Dad and she swallowed it.

Obviously, I *am* dead upset about what's happening at home, so it wasn't exactly a lie. She teased me a bit about Mr J too, but I managed to fob her off, *Who? Oh, him*, like I'd forgotten all about him.

But the truth is, it's like my mind got jetwashed clean on my birthday and the only thing that's made its way back in is him. No exaggerating, from the moment

I wake up till I go to bed, it's him, him, him. Actually, scrub that, because I dream about him all night too. 24–7 Ben Jagger on the brain.

Mum realised I didn't have my bike when I had to do the papers on foot so I had to tell her it got locked in the bike shed for the holidays. Don't know what I'll do when we go back to school, maybe say it's been nicked, which means I'll get the, 'Oh, Lara, how could you be so careless?' iPod-style guilt trips all over again, but can't think how else to explain it.

Forgot to say, got some fab pressies. Benefit make-up from Auntie Amanda and Uncle Andy, which looks brilliant on; Em got me a fab jacket from Topshop and Mum and Dad, some books and – unbelievably brilliantly – GHDs!!!

Oh, and Gran got me a candle.

A *candle*.

I've told Mum to book her in for a hearing test.

APRIL 28TH

Back to school tomorrow and I want to see him so bad it hurts.

Been sooo tempted to send him a message on

Facebook. Nearly sent him a friend request, but bottled that too. He looks so unbelievably gorgeous in his profile picture I've virtually worn my eyeballs out staring at it. But tomorrow I'll finally get to see him again in the (perfect) flesh! Feeling so excited and churned up. Suppose I get an attack of the giggles or get tongue-tied?

I can't wait to see him.

I LOVE HIM.

APRIL 29TH

Something's happened, but I don't know what.

He wasn't there when I went to the classroom first thing, and when he dashed in on the bell for registration, he didn't turn his head my way once. Then he made us watch the DVD of *Jane Eyre* in English and disappeared before I could speak to him at the end. By the time I got to the staffroom, he'd shut the door without a word. Which Mikaela saw.

The Friday school broke up, he said we were going to see Mrs Ellis together 'no arguments' and he told me his door was always open for me, but this morning, he wouldn't even *look* at me.

'Hey, Jagger Shagger,' yelled Mikaela as I walked out in the playground at lunch. 'Doesn't he love you any more, babes?' *Cackle cackle.*

I sat on my own on a bench, too miserable to even care. *Jagger Shagger.* Huh, I wish. His car was already speeding away by the time I got to the car park, even though the 4 o'clock bell was still echoing across the courtyard.

At the bus stop (RIP bike) they circled like a pack of uniformed hyenas. This morning I was invincible, but by home-time, easy prey.

'It's been so funny watching you hang round him for that stupid show,' said Molly. 'He laughs about it all the time with the other teachers, you know. Pissing themselves at Loser Lara and her stupid crush.'

'Yeah,' Chloe, Supreme Traitor, said. 'He's dead embarrassed. You can see it a mile off.'

'He was just using you to do stuff he couldn't be bothered to do and now it's finished he doesn't want to know.' Mikaela chipped in. 'He can't stand you. Nobody can.'

Sam Short-arse looked up from whatever fascinating thing he was watching on his mobile and laughed.

'No one will ever like you, Lara, so you'd better get

used to it,' Molly said. 'Oh and by the way, did you like your birthday surprise?'

Reader, I punched her.

Blood squirted out of her nose.

'Saaaam . . .' she wailed, reaching towards him, drops of blood scattering like red raindrops.

He shoved her away in disgust, shouting, 'Get OFF! Can't you see this coat is *Ralph Lauren*?'

I walked all the way home which took forever and I could hardly see where I was going, I was crying that much. I didn't show up for the papers so Mr Patel rang Mum, meaning they're both mad with me now.

Right now, I am sitting on my bed, thinking myself into a frenzy because I just don't get it. I keep rereading the entry from that night, looking for clues. There *was* something, wasn't there? The atmosphere was building in the car all the way home (has been for weeks, really) and when we looked into each other's eyes, it was like a bomb went off. He told me he thinks I'm 'amazing and unique and special'.

It is NOT me imagining this.

This REALLY happened.

So why the hell is he ignoring me now?

Later . . . I am in so much trouble. Suppose Molly's nose is broken? Mum'll lose her job soon and permanent exclusion will mean I never see HIM again. And even though he doesn't want anything to do with me, I couldn't stand that.

I want to DIE.

APRIL 30TH

I don't know how much more I can take. I'm lying in bed, trembling; trying to make sense of what's happening.

How can he do this to me? How can he make me feel like this? Bollocks to the 'sacrifices' I put myself through misery week after week, so am refusing to feel guilty about skiving one measly day, even if the exams do start tomorrow. I've done enough. It'll be OK.

Mum was dubious about leaving me on my own though. 'Are you sure you'll be all right?'

'Yeah, it's just a tummy bug. I'll be fine, honest. Go on, you're going to be late.'

'OK, but keep your mobile on and promise you'll ring me if it gets any worse? And don't forget Simon's seeing your dad, so we won't be back till half six.'

Not a tummy bug that's making me ill of course,

but my stomach is so tight and twisted, it might as well be. As soon as I heard Mum lock the front door, I lay back on my bed and settled down to wait for the phone to ring.

Expelled.

Mum and Dad would be totally fuming at first, but with no fees to pay, surely they'll be happier? I mean, no more extreme cheapskating and loads less money stress. And I seriously would work just as hard at any other school. I'll get good A level results wherever.

Assume school will let me sit my GCSEs anyway. Hopefully.

Managed to convince myself it might not be catastrophic, even started half looking forward to the call. But then my heart began to beat faster and faster until my pulse pounded *never see him again, never see him again, never see him again* and I was crying and crying and crying like I would never stop.

I was almost sick with anticipation by the afternoon, but that phone call from school never materialised.

Something else did though. Something entirely unexpected.

Bang on half past four, the doorbell rang and standing on the porch, holding my miraculously resurrected bike in one hand was Mr Jagger. Blood rushed to my head and for a second I thought I might faint. His expression changed from nervous to concerned.

'Lara, are you OK? You're as white as a sheet.'

Shock at seeing him there broke the channels of communication between my brain and my mouth. I just stood there, staring, frozen.

'I thought you'd like this back. Are your parents, I mean, is your mum in?'

'Er, no. She's at work,' I managed to stammer out.

He hesitated. 'I probably shouldn't . . . maybe I should come back later?'

Felt like I was trying to swallow gravel as I gulped, struggling to get the words out. And cold and shivery. Voice trembly.

'No, it's OK, come in.'

He dithered on the threshold, then propped the bike against the porch wall and followed me into the lounge. I gestured at the sofa and he sat down. (After he'd gone, I realised I'd given him a Royal Box view of the radiator, festooned with my drying pants. Typical.)

'Would you like a drink of something?' I desperately needed an excuse to leave to try and stop my quivery hands giving me away.

'Sit down, please. No, no, I'm fine, thanks, I can't stop. I wanted to give you your bike back today, but you weren't at school.'

I perched on the edge of the armchair, sitting on my hands. 'I'm OK. Just a tummy bug.'

'Well, I was worried about you. I know you've been through a lot recently and . . . well . . . I wanted to make sure you were all right.'

Curiouser and curiouser. How come he isn't saying anything about me being expelled?

'And your bike!' he smiled. 'My friend back home runs a bike shop. It wasn't as bad as it looked and he's made it good as new. I know how much it means to you.'

My eyes filled up. 'Thank you.'

'And . . . I . . .' He paused. 'I . . . erm . . . just wanted you to know that I appreciate all the help you gave me with the show stuff.'

'I told you, I loved doing it,' I said.

'I know, Lara. And you did a fantastic job. Hand on heart, there's no way I could have done it without you. But . . . but I think from now on perhaps you need to stop coming to find me at break-times and before school.'

My throat prickled as I stared at him.

'It's not that I don't like your company, because I do, I really do, but people . . . there have been . . . misunderstandings. Do you get what I'm saying?'

I nodded, blinking quickly.

'You've done absolutely nothing wrong. It's just people talk about what's appropriate and . . . I think you understand, don't you?' He stood up. 'So, see you in registration tomorrow, if you're over this bug?'

I nodded dumbly again, not trusting myself to speak.

'The bike shouldn't have a scratch left on it and I've had stern words with the girls today. I told them I know *everything* they've been doing. I made it extremely clear if they so much as look at you funny, I'll be straight on the phone to their parents.'

'Thanks,' I said.

He left. I locked the bike in the shed. And here I am on my own wondering whether there's any point to anything any more.

Later . . . Predictably enough, just got a late-night text from the phantom phone menace: *You shouldn't have said anything, bitch.* For once, I can't disagree. At least I know why she hasn't dobbed me in for the punch: she's shit-scared Mr J *really* knows everything.

And what 'misunderstandings'?   I   didn't 'misunderstand' anything.

He *was* going to kiss me. Why else would he look right in my eyes and lean forward?

I did NOT imagine it.

May

My head is stuck on shit spin cycle – *whirl whirl whirl*. I've got no one to talk to, no one I can turn to.

He loves me.

He loves me not.

He's a teacher, FFS! Why would he risk his whole career for a quick snog with the Queen of the Untouchables? So he was just trying to make me feel better saying all those nice things, then panicked when I misread the signals.

Stupid stupid stupid stupid stupid stupid. *That's* why he ignored me.

He froze me out all day. Perhaps he knows if people see us together they'll put two and two together. It must be crystal clear from the way I light up like a fruit machine when he's around. Makes sense for him to keep his distance. He said I was 'amazing'. You don't say that just to make someone feel better.

I feel like I'm going mad. What is it? Nearly-kiss . . . not Nearly-kiss?

And the shit keeps spinning.

Auto-piloted my way through my French oral today. I need to get a grip or I'm going to fail everything.

I couldn't help it, I sent him a private message on Facebook.

Please will you talk to me? I don't know what I've done wrong. Whatever it is, I'm sorry. Please don't ignore me. Love Lara xx

Loads later . . . My phone just pinged an email. I nearly fell out of bed in my eagerness to get it. But it was just spam inviting me to 'Try Mature Dating'.

Ha.

MAY 2ND

Today was the worst day of my life.

Mr J, Mum and Dad, Sam, Molly and that lot, exams – why can't they all give me a break?

He hasn't answered the Facebook message and it's been hours so he must've seen it by now, which means he is deliberately ignoring me. Hardly got a wink of sleep. I've been shattered since I got up. Couldn't stop checking my phone all night and still nothing. I was so exhausted I nearly put my head on the desk in the history exam. When I looked up at the clock, I'd lost half an hour. Spanish oral today too, but no idea what I said. I can't even be certain I was speaking Spanish. English lit. tomorrow, the one I most want to shine in. I know the texts inside out, but it'll still be a disaster zone. Can't revise, and sleep is impossible after the day I've had. Lying on my bed, staring up at the ceiling, that's my limit.

Why? Because THEY have started up again and just when I thought I knew what to expect, they find new tortures to try. It was the worst it's ever been today.

When I got up this morning, Mum took one look at the rain lashing the kitchen window and said, 'You're not riding your bike in this.'

I shivered at the bus stop, and not only because I got soaked through. The journey there was no problem – light to moderate verbal abuse is like water off a duck's back to me now. But at 4 o'clock that lot surrounded me. Of all the days for the home-time bus to be delayed . . .

'Hello, Lara,' said Sam. 'You never did answer my question, did you?'

Before I even had chance to figure out what he was on about, I was propelled into the shadows of the churchyard. A hand clamped my mouth shut while someone else grabbed my hair and pulled it so hard my eyes started streaming. Sam yanked my blazer off and my cardie fell open. I struggled desperately, but two of his mates were straitjacketing my arms so I was stuck, helpless. And Sam didn't stop there; I heard Molly's nasty giggle as the buttons pinged off my shirt into the air. He ripped it wide open.

'Hmmm. Interesting,' Sam said. 'You *do* wear a bra then, Titless. Er, what for exactly?'

Then he tugged it completely up, leaving my whole chest naked. Frantically twisting my body round to hide myself from all those eyes just got me Mikaela snarling in my ear, 'Keep still or you'll get more than that.'

Then Molly joined in and snatched at my ponytail

so hard she must've pulled a clump out by the roots. I strained against the arms that held me as the flashes of camera phones lit up my exposed skin, but they were far too strong.

'You shouldn't have hit me, you fucking bitch,' she said, her fingers so tight to my scalp my eyes were streaming. 'You've made it a whole load worse for yourself. Say anything about me to Jagger or anyone again and I will make sure your mum gets it.'

'I don't care!' I shouted, wriggling like a fish caught on a hook. 'I don't care if you make up some story. No one's going to believe you anyway.'

'So what? Even if they believe you and I get bollocked for it, do you think my mum and dad will still want her working for them? Or their friends? Or at their office? Face it, Titless, there's nothing you can do. Not if you want your mum to have a job.'

She was right of course. *Checkmate.*

'Quick!' shouted Sam as the bus rumbled round the bend.

'By the time I've finished with you, you're going to wish you were dead,' said Molly, almost scalping me with a final vicious tug.

The ones holding my arms flung me forward on to a

gravestone and they all legged it. I pulled my ruined shirt around me and buttoned my blazer up, then scrabbled for my bag. But I was crying so hard I couldn't find it for ages.

I set off in the pouring rain and when I finally got home, Mum had a go at me for missing the bus, which, to be honest, I could've done without as my head was absolutely killing me. Missed the papers too, so I let Mr Patel down yet again, which means, nice though he is, he'll probably give me the sack now.

Couldn't even face going to karate in case I bumped into any of them in town. My bedroom is starting to feel like the only place I am safe.

Or a prison cell.

Oh God, what can I do?

I can't avoid them, especially now Mr J doesn't let me anywhere near him, but I am so sick of spending every day looking over my shoulder ready for the next attack. And how can I go back to school knowing all those people saw my naked chest? My head's killing me and my shoulders are agony from being wrenched nearly out of their sockets. Oh yeah and my exams are a DISASTER.

Molly's right, I do wish I was dead.

Later . . . The anonymous texter has just sent me a video clip of the whole thing and I know I won't be the only one who's got it.

The only consolation is that because it was so rainy and chaotic, the images aren't that clear; you'd only really know it was me from the people chanting 'tit-less, tit-less' in the background. But not much of a consolation really.

I have done NOTHING to deserve this. I know I said a couple of mean things to Sam that time, about his height and his dandruff or whatever, but it was in self-defence. And I only hit Molly because she smashed up my bike.

They started it. They are psychopaths.

Going back to bed now to pray for decent weather tomorrow. Come on, weather, please please please don't make me have to catch the bus.

MAY 3RD

Still no answer from Mr J.

I must have checked Facebook a thousand times now, praying there'd be one, but nothing. Given up now anyway. I was wrong: he doesn't care about me.

I can't be arsed to put the detail about how school

went today. Molly's jibes, Mr Jagger's blanking me, people sniggering. In the lit. exam, the words on the page swam until I couldn't even read the questions. Epic epic fail.

I had a massive headache all day from dehydration: daren't even have a sip of water now in case I need the toilet. The only vaguely saving thing was that Mrs Murphy letting me hide out in the library at lunchtime.

After I'd fed and watered Simon tonight, I locked myself in the bathroom with every paracetamol I could lay my hands on. Tipped them out on the floor. Counted.

Fifteen.

Plenty.

I stared at them for ages and when I'd finally made my mind up, Simon came banging on the door all hysterical, shouting, 'My wee is coming out!' so I had to quickly put them back in the bottle.

If I had an en suite, it'd all be over now.

MAY 6TH

Had definitive proof of how little Mum and Dad know me when they gave me the 'Netmums Guide to Familicide (maybe): Step 1 – Allaying your Teenager's

Fears' lecture when I got home tonight.

I'd completely forgotten my 'family annihilation' meltdown the other night, what with all the other stuff that's been going on, but they evidently think that's why I've been so quiet lately. They're too wrapped up in their own lovelorn-ness to see my heart's been smashed to pieces too.

No sooner had I parked the bike up (thank you for the sunshine, God/Nature/Whoever) than Mum flung the back door open. 'Ah, there you are, love. Come in, your dad's here.'

I honestly can't remember the last time I saw them both smiling while in the same room and under any other circumstances I would have been v. pleased, but the atmosphere was disturbing.

'We know it's upsetting having Dad move out,' said Mum with a fake everything's-going-to-be-just-peachy grin.

'Yes,' said Dad, 'but it's not forever.' Mum shot him a glance, which he totally ignored. 'And I'm fine, love, honestly. It's a sad situation, but I'm coping. You don't need to worry about that.'

What a relief to be able to cross *Dad going insane in the membrane* off the stress list.

They went on a bit about why they'd split up, but I already knew it all from listening in on their endless rows (not that I told them that of course). Then Dad went back to the 'grotty bedsit' and Mum went back to looking miserable. I went to karate and thought about punching Molly and Mr Jagger.

PS Not punching him, thinking about him. I still love him even though he's killing me.

PPS Biology AND chemistry back to back today. The worst day of all. I don't know why I even bothered turning up.

MAY 8TH

Cambridge meeting after school. I double-checked no one I know is going, but as I suspected, it's mainly geeky Year 12s from the boys' school, mostly strangers. Except Mr Jagger of course, who might as well be.

The trip sounds interesting, which is something, I suppose. We leave at nine on the Monday and should be back by teatime on Wednesday. There's going to be a tour of the campus and talks from previous students as well as the sample lectures. Mrs Torrens explained everything – apparently she does this every year with Mrs Muirhouse. Mr Jagger looked through me like I was made of glass. I can't even look at him, knowing he didn't answer my message. Obviously, he thinks I'm too much of a freak show to bother with.

MAY 10TH

Popped in on Gran after the papers. She was in a foul mood as she handed me the dirty laundry bag for Mum, saying crossly, 'Tell her not to Vanish my gussets this time. My undercarriage has been on fire all week.'

Mental image I did *not* need.

Should've hit the revision hard when I got back. (Spanish written next. Might be OK, *dedos cruzados*, I got an A* in the mock.) But instead turned my room into a jumble sale.

Doesn't matter. According to Mum I keep all my clothes on the floordrobe anyway. I've been trying to decide what to take to Cambridge, which is proving to be an impossible, headache-inducing task: my whole wardrobe is a giant malfunction.

I wish Emma was here. She's amazing at stuff like

this, a proper fashion fairy. She can sling on any old rag and *abracadabra* it looks like it cost a bomb, plus she actively *enjoys* being a skinny red-head. And she is even entirely at ease with the Surname of Shame. Sigh. How does she do it?

Wardrobe Inventory
Two pairs supermarket jeans, both too short
Five pairs of black/navy/grey leggings all of which
have gone only minorly cobwebby on the bum
Various formerly-white tops
A black cardie from Emma
Topshop jacket (ditto)
Denim skirt (ditto)
School shoes? Trainers? Slippers?

And this sad ragbag is what's left after I've already culled the worst offenders. I'm going to look like I covered myself in glue and ran through Oxfam. There's no way round it – the iPod-replacement-fund-replacing-the-bike-fund will have to go on hold so I can go clothes shopping for the trip.

I was dead excited about going to Cambridge before, but now if I could back out this minute, I 100% would.

He still hasn't spoken to me and I can't help thinking it'd be infinitely preferable to spend no time at all with him than have him freeze me out like this.

Every time I think about it, it feels as if I'm choking. I thought he really liked me and all the time he just felt sorry for me.

Later . . . My mind is a cinema screen playing the same film over and over. We're in the car, we look at each other, he leans towards me, the horn goes, we jump apart. We're in the car, we look at each other, the horn goes, we jump apart . . .

I am so confused.

MAY 12TH

Torture is banned under the terms of the Geneva Convention, right? OK then, how is Mr Ben Jagger of Huddersfield Girls' High School getting away with it?

I mean, yeah, he's not exactly wiring electrodes to my foof or pulling out my fingernails with rusty pliers, but what he *is* doing is a million times worse. Physical pain I could handle, but this blanking me is the worst kind of torture imaginable. I love him with my whole heart and he acts like I don't exist.

If only my brain had an off switch. Can't stop thinking about the Nearly-kiss and the more I think about it, the more I think it *was* going to be a kiss. And then I think it wasn't.

Yes no yes no flip flop flip flop.

Please can someone teach me how to not think? (How do *you* do it, Mikaela?).

The Case For:

- If he was going for the glovebox/door, why did he leap away?
- He said I was gorgeous/special/amazing, etc.
- The *frisson*.

The Case Against:

- He's a teacher.
- I'm his pupil.
- He's human perfection.
- I'm Lara Titliss.

Lunchtimes are nail-bitingly tense now I'm banned from his room, but even so the witches have been keeping their distance. I don't understand it. They've had opportunities, like today at break, I walked past them on the way to the exam hall. There they were, a coven in a huddle round Molly's iPad, no one else around. I braced myself for the onslaught when . . . nothing except a few snidey sniggers.

Maybe they've hired a hitman and he's just waiting for a window in his schedule. Or maybe they've realised that exposing my tits to the world was going too far.

In my dreams.

I've watched enough horror films to know there's always an eerie calm before the storm.

MAY 13TH

Right, firstly and foremost, there will be absolutely no mention of HIM. This is a He Who Shall Not Be Named free zone. There is to be no further worrying about HIM, speculation about HIS state of mind or comment on the pain caused by HIS continued disregard of me. Or the fact he still hasn't answered my stupid FB message.

I wish I'd never sent it. I have had a stern word with myself and am going to pull myself together before we go to Cambridge.

Emma emailed me links to clothes she's bought

over the past couple of months because (apart from her playing Beauty to my Beast) we're pretty similar so if it suits her, it'll suit me. Even though I feel guilty splurging the whole iPod fund on clothes (die, Molly, die), I absolutely must look AMAZING and SPECIAL and BEAUTIFUL on this trip.

And if HE continues to act like I don't exist, well, maybe *someone* will notice me. Not talking specifically about boys, because my heart belongs to HIM and HIM alone, can't avoid that. But *someone*. There's got to be more to life than being miserable and lonely all the time. I want to meet people I like who won't act as if I'm an untouchable. I want to feel that I *belong*, even if it is only for a couple of days.

Compulsively watching YouTube make-up tutorials at the mo, picking up top tips. Eyebrow pencil is quite a revelation when you've had invisibrows for the last sixteen years. Somewhere between 'bad Botox' and 'Star Trek cosplay' initially, but I've nailed 'I am ginger, but with eyebrows' now.

Plus Emma uses temporary foam dyes on her hair to pimp her ginge, so I'm going to give that a go later. I need to learn to love my hair the way she does. Before Mum started trimming it with the kitchen scissors (i.e.

back when we could afford salons), hairdressers always used to go, 'Ooh, you've got lovely hair, so long and thick!' But I'm no fool, I recognise it was a) a tactful manoeuvre to avoid mentioning the 'G' word and b) buttering me up for a tip.

I suppose if human eyes saw in monochrome, my hair might be passable. It's the screaming carroty-ness people seem to have an issue with. Dress me in black-and-white stripes and I could body-double a Belisha beacon. Emma reckons it's a gift, but it's felt more like a curse to me, with the comments I've had over the years.

Anyway, the shopping list looks like this:

One jumper and two tops from H&M
Skirt from Primark
Boots from Primark
Jeans from Topshop (expensive, but worth it for the
    leg length, Em reckons)

That's the easy bit. It's deciding which colours clash least with my hair that's giving me the grief, but hopefully a dyeing sesh should help if it tones it down. And as I always buy clothes two sizes too big to disguise my beanpole physique, whatever I wear looks like a sack. Emma made me promise to buy things that fit.

'I would say show off your best features and play down your flaws,' she told me. 'But you haven't got any flaws. You're built like a supermodel.'

Yeah, right. And if Vivienne Westwood ever starts designing ironing-board covers, call my agent.

I haven't bought any new clothes for ages, quite excited now. Not that I'm trying to impress anyone or anything. Course not. Who could *I* possibly want to impress?!

PS Still not thinking about HIM. (Good.)

MAY 15TH

Town was dead quiet so I managed not to bump into anyone from school. Result! Also turned out to be an excellent shopping mission. Got a shirt from H&M, cream and black, sort of Victorian looking (must be all that *Jane Eyre*). Superskinnies from Topshop (if you've got it, etc.). Black 'pleather' knee-length boots that'll work with jeans or a skirt; a black jumper with white stars on it from Primark and a couple of cheap-as-chips scarves to wear with those plain white tops I've already got.

After I'd spent up on the clothes budget, went to Superdrug intending to grab the hair dye and head home, but ended up inhaling their complete aftershave collection. I swear the snooty-faced assistant was about to ring a substance abuse helpline. *Three times* I told her I didn't need any help. Anyway, I worked out he wears Hermès; one sniff and my knees buckled. I drenched myself in it and, like the hopeless case I am, have been sniffing my scarf ever since I got home. Now attempting to suppress the urge to sleep with it under my pillow, but it smells so good . . .

Jury's still out on whether the dye job was a success. Mum came in halfway through, not in the best of moods.

'Good Lord, it's like a halal slaughterhouse in here!'

She fetched the towel we dry Paddington off with and so my hair has stunk of wet dog all night.

'And clear up that mess. I'm not going to tell you again.'

'Is that a promise?' I said under my breath and ran into my bedroom before she could respond.

Spent about an hour scrubbing the grout behind the sink with a toothbrush. Fun way to spend a Saturday night, eh? And for future reference, it is a big mistake to ignore the advice on 'staining'. (Unless the desired result is 'Holby City head injuries special' in which case expect very convincing results.)

PS 1. Number of times I have thought about Mr Jagger this week: 604,800

2. Number of times he has spoken to me: five (Registration. Him: Lara? Me: Here, Sir.)

Coincidentally, question one is also the answer to 'how many seconds are there in a week?'

MAY 16TH

Twelve hours to go . . .

The Cambridge countdown continues. I've tried all the clothes on in different combinations, practised the make-up, GHD-ed my hair and it's official: I am hot to trot.

When I went downstairs at teatime, Simple Simon said, 'You look really weird,' which confirms I'm looking gorgeous because, well, he's a six-year-old boy and therefore knows NOTHING. Even Mum stepped out from the shadow of her gloom-cloud long enough to tell me I look lovely.

I googled 'hair dye stains' and it recommended lemon juice. No lemon in the Titliss fruit bowl (we're not that kind of family), but there was a squeezy bottle left over from Pancake Day and it seems to have worked. I look less like I've been in an accident at any rate. Washed it again and the water's faded to shades of beetroot wee, so I reckon even if it chucks it down, I should be colourfast.

So Cambridge tomorrow.

Some wise bloke once said the longest journey begins with a single step. Who knows? Maybe this trip will be my first crap totter on the road to fabulousness. How do I feel? Hmmmm, well, the studious part of me is looking forward to the lectures and finding out more. (And trying to calm the panicky inner squawky voice going, 'You didn't revise enough! You won't be doing A levels, never mind going to uni!')

But the whole truth is I'm torn in two: half of me is still unbelievably hyped at the thought of being with HIM for three whole days. If he does genuinely enjoy my company, like he said, and his only real concern is 'the way people talk', then being away from school will make it OK, won't it? With different surroundings, we can go back to how we were. I miss him.

I know if I told anyone, they'd say it's just a crush and I'll get over him, or some equally patronising platitude. But I know for an absolute FACT that he is my soulmate. We're Romeo and Juliet, destined to be together, forced apart by circumstances. And I realise I sound like a melodramatic twelve-year-old, but I am not apologising. This is how I feel. My heart is shouting it at me: I love him.

But then the next minute, I'm almost doubled up with nerves. Suppose he ignores me on the trip? Suppose he *was* just being nice to me all this time and I read too much into it? What if he hasn't actually realised yet that we are soulmates?

I don't know if I can take any more pain.

Later . . . Went down to make a quick fromage à la toast for supper and got into *another* ridiculous cleaning row with Mum. She needs to take a CHILL PILL. Mr Jagger, even if you invisiblise me for the whole trip, it'll be well worth it to escape her endless nagging.

Mum: I can't believe the state of this kitchen!

Me: What state?

Mum: (brandishing a tea towel) *Smack!* Crumbs everywhere! *Smack!* Breakfast dishes in the sink! Is it not enough you've wrecked the bathroom? And cheese! *Smack!* Melted cheese all over the cooker. I give up on you, Lara, I really do.

Me: Tell you what, Mum, shall I kill myself? Would that make you happy?

Mum: No, not particularly. (folding up tea towel and putting it in drawer) But if you *do* decide to do a Sylvia Plath, take the Mr Muscle in with you.

I'M AN OPPRESSED TEENAGER – GET ME OUT OF HERE!

Thank God for C-Day: eleven hours, twenty-three minutes and counting.

Mum's comment got me thinking about the fifteen paracetamols and how she's no idea that isn't really a joke. Even now it's on my mind. If I hadn't got interrupted, I would definitely have taken them. I'm only here today because Simon needed a wee.

Bizarre.

I owe my life to a Fruit Shoot.

MAY 17TH

Right at this minute I'm in my dorm room IN CAMBRIDGE hanging around, waiting for the three girls from another school who are supposed to be sharing it, so while I've got some time to kill, I'll scribble down the story so far.

Took ages to get here, but as I haven't got an iPod any more (die, Molly, die) and reading on buses makes me spew, I had no option but to spend the whole journey focusing on the back of Mr Jagger's head.

My stomach was full of acrobatic butterflies at first, but he only said 'hello', nothing else. He noticed I looked really different out of uniform though. I *think* so anyway. I mean, he must've. I had the skinny jeans and the boots on with a lacy blouse on top, and he must at least have been surprised by my hair.

I hadn't really seen it in daylight properly before, it's not what you'd call subtle. People have been throwing buckets of water over me, reaching for the fire extinguishers, etc. But it does look really, really good. Glamorous.

Some of the other kids definitely did a double-take; I recognised two Hellbus boys (ones I've never spoken to) looking well shocked so I must be making an impact. If they could recognise the new me, then Mr J must've done, right?

Later . . . Had to stop because the other girls arrived. They seemed nice enough, but they definitely did that 'let's work out how posh you are' scan and on the class-o-meter I rate a very low 'low'. So while Araminta ('call me Minty'), Satvinder ('call me Satty') and Francesca ('call me Fanny'. Yes, *really*) traded polo pony and yacht tales, I sat on the bed and pretended to read *Hard Times*.

There's that kind of confidence rich, privileged people have that I will never, ever have. And for all her VB jeans and Mulberry bags, even Molly would feel a proper slob surrounded by these glowy posh girls. I could hardly mutter a word for fear of being heckled over my accent and when they did try to talk to me (and they were nice enough to do that) I'm not sure they actually understood what I said when they asked me where I came from.

'Huddersfield.'

Blank faces.

'In the Pennines.'

'Oh, *the north*'

'Off the M62.'

Blank faces.

'The motorway that runs between Liverpool and Hull.'

Or maybe I said the intergalactic stargate linking Pluto to Uranus.

Cambridge is a different world, Mr J said. Well, I can't argue with that. The city, the architecture, the grounds – even the grass in the courtyard is literally greener than the stuff we have at home.

The girls have gone to meet their chums now in the (irony) 'common room', but I'm staying put a while longer.

Don't make me laugh, Mr J. For all you go on about a level academic playing field, it's nothing to do with having the smarts really, is it? It's having the right accent, the right parents, the right background. None of which applies to me.

I feel like a goldfish entered for the Grand National.

Even later . . . Confession Time and also an opportunity to bin the chip on my shoulder. (Maybe for 'chip' read 'five kilos of King Edwards'.)

Reading back over earlier, I think I was really harsh on my roomies. Feel mean now, as they were dead friendly, trying to draw me into the conversation and everything. V. interesting too, i.e. wanted to talk about more than the boys' school and where they do the best fake tan, which makes a change from 11G's fave topics.

Bumped into Mr J on the way out of the dining room and we had some awkward chit-chat about the food, which was bizarrely loads worse than having him ignore me because now he's treating me like just another student when I'm so not. The way he is with me now *hurts*.

Better go now, the girls are back and we're going to a Brontë lecture. I know HE'LL be there too.

I wish love was a tap you could just shut off when you're done.

Really loads later on . . .

Oh my God!!! I can't believe what has happened. I need to get this down on paper while it's still fresh in my mind.

Who am I kidding?

I will NEVER forget a single second of this evening, not if I live to be one hundred, dribbling and incontinent in a care home.

It's dead late now – 1.30? 2? – but I can't wait till tomorrow so have sneaked out to the bathroom to try to write this without waking the girls in the dorm. No doubt whatsoever: in the PowerPoint presentation of my life so far, the best slides will be taken from what happened tonight.

The dinner-is-served bell rang at six and I went downstairs to the refectory (poshspeak for 'canteen') with Minty, Satty and (teeheehee) Fanny, discussing the lectures, feeling like a proper student. We'd gone ultra-glam too: Minty has her eye on a lad she sat next to in Introduction to the Gothic and I, well, no mystery why I dolled myself up.

The room was laid out with long trestle-style tables and benches à la Hogwarts and, lo and behold, Mr Jagger was sitting on the same one as us. 'Your teacher is DROP-DEAD GORGEOUS!' said Minty under her breath. Well, duh. You don't need a degree from Cambridge to spot that.

I wasn't looking too shabby myself, kept catching admiring glances from various boys around the room. But it barely even registered, because when Ben is around no one else exists. Anyway, I was away from the troubles at home, talking to people who genuinely seemed to like me and all of this under his gaze. I was almost happy for the first time since the night of my birthday.

Then (like it always does when my life seems on track for two minutes) things went poo-shaped. Some of the others from our group were at the table too, including the boys from the Hellbus. We hadn't even got through the soup course when I noticed one of them (Barney?) staring at me. He started whispering to the other one (Chris?) and nodding in my direction. Next, as Chris/Barney started fiddling with his phone, a shot of adrenalin hit me in the ribs and I *knew* they were watching one of Sam's horror movies.

Mr Jagger spotted them. 'Hand it over, lads. You know the rules, not at the table.' *Horror.*

As he took the phone out of Chris/Barney's hand, he automatically glanced at the screen. I felt my face burn as he did a double take, then stared, witnessing one of my multiple humiliations unfolding in front of him. After a few terrible, endless seconds, he looked up and straight at me.

My chair clattered to the floor, loud as a gunshot, instantly silencing the dinnertime hubbub. As I bolted for the door, he shouted, 'Lara! Wait!' but I carried on into the cool night, running away from the college grounds with his footsteps echoing behind. How could I face him, knowing what he'd just seen? But I was racing blindly down unfamiliar streets, nowhere to go and within a minute I'd run straight up a dead end.

'Bloody hell,' he gasped, hands on his knees, when he caught me. 'Thought about trying out for the next Olympics?' He stood up straight. 'Come on. Let's go and have a proper chat away from prying eyes. We need to sort this out.'

What else could I do? I shrugged, too embarrassed to utter a word, and followed him back on to the main street towards the lights on the corner.

'We can go in here,' he said.

The pub was quiet, just a few groups of students huddled round tables. Steamy fug misted up the windows by the booth where Mr Jagger left me while he went to the bar. He slid a glass of Coke across the table at me and took a sip of his lager.

'So, do you want to tell me what's going on?'

I was on my own with him in a pub, everyone assuming he was my boyfriend. Literally, this was a dream come true, but all I could do was bite my lip and cringe inside, wishing a trapdoor would open beneath me, thinking, DID YOU SEE MY BOYBOOBS???

But he read my mind. 'You know, I didn't catch the details, but it's obviously serious. Tell me, I can help.'

He took another slurp while I jiggled the ice in my glass. Here in Cambridge, in this pub alone with him,

Molly's threats shrivelled to the empty words of a distant bully, nothing more.

Where to start?

'So you know you said you spoke to Molly that day I was off school? Well, here, look.' I passed him my phone. Frowning, he started to flick through the anonymous messages, reading them quickly.

'And,' deep breath, 'there's more.'

He looked at me and it was weird. I was poised for my epic meltdown involving wailing, gnashing of teeth, etc. but . . . nothing. I could've been relating the plot of a book I'd read instead of releasing months of misery. Eerily calm.

His face passed through shock to concern to anger when I finished up with the tale of my unwilling topless debut. I guess that's what he glimpsed on Chris/Barney's phone.

'You must know that's a serious assault, and to film it . . .' He put his hand on mine and gave it a gentle squeeze. 'It is an actual prosecutable offence. Why on earth didn't you tell me before?'

'I didn't think you'd want to know,' I said quietly.

He sat back in his chair and stared at his drink, silent for a while, then went, 'OK, because of what I said the day I brought your bike round. I get that. But Jesus, Lara, why didn't you tell your mum?'

'Because my mum works for Molly's parents. She said if I ever dobbed her in, she'd get my mum the sack.'

'The devious little – That's rubbish. You need to tell your mum as soon as we get back, and if you don't then I will. How many times do I have to tell you that you don't need to put up with this before you start believing me?'

'I can't. PLEASE don't say anything to anyone,' I said.

You don't know the half of it. Mum's stress, Dad leaving, the money pressure over school – I laid my home problems on the table alongside my bullying woes. And unlike the night of the Nearly-kiss, I held nothing back.

'Oh God, I had no idea. You poor girl.' He drained the last of his drink. 'Bloody hell, I think I need another pint after that. Do you want a Coke?'

'Yes, please,' I said.

There's no way I can sleep now, but it's got nothing to do with the caffeine overdose. It's what happened next that's keeping me wide awake. I watched him walk back from the bar, the peaceful sensation still there. Almost surreal how detached I was.

In a pub discussing footage of my naked norks with Mr J.

No biggie.

Mr J or shock: *something* was detraumatising the situation.

'I think I owe you an explanation.' He took a long swallow of his lager. 'That day I brought your bike back, and then afterwards, it was, I don't know . . .' He covered his face with his hands for a second then placed them flat down on the table. 'Difficult. It was difficult to know the right thing to do. Do you understand what I'm getting at?'

Ish. I nodded.

'Then your message on Facebook – the same thing. I wanted to answer, but the teacher / student social-media issue is a can of worms and so . . .'

He tailed off. I sipped my coke and waited.

'So I didn't answer, panicked, I suppose. And looking back, that was a bad decision. I thought keeping my distance was for the best, but instead I've let you suffer all this alone and made it a whole heap worse. But it was never my intention, I swear. It was because . . .'

He paused. *One second. Two seconds.*

'Because of what?' I prompted.

Then he told me.

When he finished, I just stared, processing the

words. The way he'd been acting the past few weeks was now presented to me from a totally different angle. One which made COMPLETE sense. He said Mrs Ellis had called him into her office for 'a chat' before school on the first day back after Easter. The cleaner had been in to say she'd seen us alone a few times in the classroom after school and the caretaker had seen me get in the car. Mrs Ellis explained she knew it was entirely innocent, but she warned him to avoid 'situations that could be open to misinterpretation'.

So he hadn't been blanking me through choice; he'd been *told* to do it.

'Time, please, ladies and gentlemen,' called the barman as he jangled the brass bell behind the bar. I saw the pub had emptied without us noticing and Ben knocked into the table as he got to his feet, jogging the empty pint glasses into a chorus of clinks.

'We'd better get you back. It's an early start tomorrow and look at you, you haven't even got a coat. Here, put this on.' He slipped his jacket over my shoulders, the heat from his body still warm on the leather. Wrapped up, enveloped in the smell of him, I was impervious to the chill in the air as we walked back to the college.

'I meant every word I said in the car that night.'

He stopped and took hold of my hand. It was dark and deserted on the narrow cobbled street and the street lights cast a gentle glow on us. 'I hate the way those kids have made you feel so down on yourself. You need to believe you're a special girl. Very special. You look absolutely stunning tonight.'

The *frisson*!

Suddenly it was back, crackling in the air between us. He looked at me, I looked at him and it was like a replay of that night in his car four weeks ago, except this time it actually happened.

A kiss. A passionate, real kiss that echoed through my whole body and made my head whirl.

He broke away first. 'Oh God, sorry. I shouldn't have done that.'

'It's OK,' I said.

He put his hand up to his forehead and sighed loudly. 'No, it's not OK. You've got so much stress in your life and I'm bringing you more. What an idiot.' He walked off a few paces, then turned back round.

'That'll teach me to drink on the job. What a lightweight.' I moved towards him, but he backed away, hands up defensively. 'I'm sorry.'

The nights I'd dreamt of this and now he was

apologising?! Seeing him so nervous made me suddenly brave. Reckless.

Now or never, now or never . . .

I took hold of both his hands and pulled him so close our faces were just centimetres apart.

'But I *want* it to happen again,' I whispered, looking straight into his eyes. And I cupped his face and kissed him. Weeks of longing and misery were in that kiss. Every drop of emotion in my body transmitted through my lips to his.

He kept his arms round my shoulders and we stayed like that, holding each other, while time went on around us. Not saying anything, just being there, together.

'We need to get back,' he said eventually and I realised I was shivering, despite his jacket.

The college was spookily quiet. With the closed curtains like sleeping eyes, only the dim lights of the quadrangle were there to guide us to the entrance. The place looked the same as when I'd raced out of the dining room only a couple of hours earlier, but my whole life had changed since then. *I'd* changed.

At the foot of the dorm staircase, he took his arm from round my shoulder and I shrugged off his coat. We swapped mobile numbers before one last kiss.

'Lara . . .' He hesitated. 'Lara, you know how much trouble we could get into if you tell anyone about this. People twist things . . .'

'I understand,' I said quickly. 'Don't worry, of course I won't tell anyone.'

He hugged me and I watched as he walked away across the courtyard. And here I am now, writing this in the bathroom. The rest of the world is asleep and I'm on a cloud so high, I don't know how I'll ever come back down.

Mr Jagger – *Ben* – kissed me. Really kissed me.

He wasn't ignoring me, he had no choice.

It's my turn to be a tiger not a sheep. From now on, I'm doing what's right for me and nothing and no one in my life is more important than him.

And if that upsets people, then tough tits.

MAY 18TH

Woke up panicking. Suppose it's like the last time? One minute cosy-cosy in the car, the next doors shut in my face. Am I in for the silent treatment again?

NO!

A text: *Morning. How are you? B*

Good thanks. You? L

Bit groggy, but OK. You going down to breakfast now?

Yep. See you there?

OK x

A text kiss and it's only 7.30 which means I must've been the first thing he thought of when he woke up! Better get ready now. Going for the black boots over skinny jeans, black star jumper on top; make-up to look grown-up but not done-up; sesh with the miracle that is GHDs, then down to the dining room where I'll see him.

Ben.

Later . . . I've grabbed five minutes upstairs before lunch. He winked at me at breakfast when no one was looking, but he had to be discreet, so he couldn't do anything else. Really obvious he was as desperate to talk as I was.

Wah! Still can't believe Mr J kissed me!

Physically clenching my fists to prevent my rebellious fingers texting Emma. Most exciting news in the history of news and it's something I can't share with her.

Had anticipated oddness from the roomies *re* my sudden exodus last night. Luckily, in their capacity as the world's nicest girls, they were all sympathy and loveliness. (*Drifting off into daydream where they suddenly move up north and join 11G.*) Sigh. Not nosy or snarky and I convinced them 'boy trouble' was at the heart of it. Which is the truth, sort of. (Well, if you swap 'boy' for 'man' and 'trouble' for 'amazingness'.) And as for the pair of Hellbus tossers, I think Mr J (Ben!) must've had a word: they completely avoided even glancing my way.

Lectures were interesting. Er, probably. To be honest, I've got my mind so firmly on the romantic present that the romantic poets have no chance. Hope he wants to go back to the pub tonight. Maybe I can even persuade him to let me have a proper drink.

Must. Stop. Checking. My. Phone. I'm not texting first. I'm not texting first. I'm not texting first.

Loads later . . . Wow, wow and then some more wow!

Bathroom floor déjà vu. It's 1.30 and I need to write tonight down right now. Can't hold off till the morning in case a tiny detail slips away.

Checking my phone every ten seconds didn't make any messages materialise and when the little envelope icon finally flashed my heart leapt then plummeted. Wasn't from him, it was Mum, checking things were all right.

I had nibbled my nails to the bone before I felt it vibrate in my pocket again.

How are you? Bx

Good. You? Lx

Not bad. You up for another drink? x

Yes, then I'll become your love slave, worship you for the rest of eternity and have your babies.

No, Lara! Delete! Delete!

Sure. What time? Lx

Meet you outside the gate 8.30. OK? Bx

See you then. x

'We know your secret,' said (teeheehee) Fanny in a sing-song tone as we tramped up to the dorm together after dinner. Satty and Minty nodded and smirked in unison.

My insides dropped so hard I'm surprised they didn't hear the *clang* as they hit the floor. 'S-secret?'

'You've met a hot guy from one of the other schools, haven't you? Go on, do tell all, we're *dying* to know.'

Phew. 'What makes you think that?'

Satty joined in. 'Well, the way you were out till the wee small hours last night. And of course your, erm, *souvenir.*'

'My what?'

'Souvenir. As in the irrefutable evidence of your amorous rendezvous.' She wafted her hand in a circle round her chin.

Ah, snog rash.

Anyway, I've let them believe in 'hot guy from another school' (generally acting coy when they ask for the goss) while I'm EXPLODING with the need to share. But I have to keep it buttoned, for obvious reasons.

'Where are you off to now? I mean, I take it you're not joining us in the common room this evening,' said Minty, raising her eyebrows as I pulled on my boots and gave my hair a final swish in the mirror.

'Oh, nowhere special.'

'Well, you'll make "nowhere special" look *très* glam, darling.'

'Seriously? Cheers!'

'You're bloody gorgeous!' She gazed ruefully down at her own curvy body. 'What I wouldn't give for your legs.'

'There's nothing wrong with your own legs!'

'Thank you, sweetie,' she said. 'But there's no ignoring it: I'll always be a carthorse not a racehorse. Whereas you . . .' She swept her arm towards me. 'You, darling, are 100% thoroughbred.'

How lovely is that? I gave her a hug. 'I think that's the nicest thing anyone's ever said to me. And you are *so* not a carthorse.'

I strode out to meet Ben feeling ten feet tall and insanely proud of every inch. Took deep breaths as a precaution while I walked across the quadrangle, but when I saw him silhouetted against the gate, his film-star looks still made me go all wobbly. Then he put his arm round me and it felt like the most natural thing in the world.

Back in the same pub as last night, we talked non-stop. He wouldn't let me have a proper drink, so I was on the Cokes again. But who needs alcohol when they've got love in their veins?

'Won't Mr McGeorge and Mrs Torrens wonder where you've got to?' I asked.

He gave me a funny look. 'Can you keep a secret?'

'Of course.'

'Promise you won't tell.'

'Cross my heart.'

He smiled. 'Well, they're a bit too busy with each other to notice what I'm up to. If you catch my drift.'

'No way! Mr McGeorge and Mrs Torrens are having a . . .?'

'Yep,' he continued. 'But that is strictly confidential, OK?'

'My lips are sealed.'

But bleurgh! They're so *old*.

I swear I could listen to Ben talk 24-7 for the rest of my days and it still wouldn't be enough. The things he's done, the places he's been – only a few years older than me and his life's already been a five-course banquet whereas mine's been a soggy cheese sandwich. He's travelled to places I've never even heard of. The most exciting thing that's ever happened to me is meeting him.

It was on the tip of my tongue to confess that, but I didn't. Don't want to make him think I'm some stalkery sadcase. And what I said ages ago about us being on the same wavelength? So true. Super-spooky how he's totally tuned into my thoughts.

'I know how it feels when you think the world is against you. You and me, we're the same.'

Then he told me stuff from when he was at school. So weird, we've been through the same things. He utterly understands where I'm coming from. *He* was bullied at school. *His* mum and dad split up when he was my age.

'I know it sounds stupid . . .' he said, then smiled and looked at his drink. 'Oh, never mind.'

'Go on,' I said.

'No, you'll laugh,' he said, peeping up at me through his fringe, dead cute and young.

'I won't. Promise.'

'Well, I kind of feel like getting the contract at school when you're going through such a hard time there was meant to happen. So I can help you.'

'No,' I said. 'That doesn't sound stupid at all.'

And it doesn't. Without him, I would have had nothing to live for the past few months. Not being melodramatic either. It's true.

He pulled me into a shop doorway on the walk back. Admittedly, not the most glamorous of locations, but the dim street lights and the beautiful buildings cast a glimmer over the scene that turned it into a romantic film set. Anyway, by that point he could've dragged me inside a septic tank and I wouldn't have given a monkey's.

When we finally came up for air, he stroked my hair and held me in his arms.

'Oh, Lara, Lara, Lara. What have you done to me?' he sighed.

'Done in a good way or a bad way?' I asked, loving the way he was kissing the top of my head in between the words.

'Bit of both. Good you, bad – no, TERRIBLE – situation. The trouble we could get into over this, but I haven't been able to stop thinking about you for weeks.'

Was I hearing this right?

'Did you cast a spell on me?' he continued.

'Not intentionally,' I replied, then, because hey, who wouldn't ask? 'So what exactly have you been thinking, you know, about me?'

'Oh, how you're beautiful and clever and great company and funny. How you're so unbelievably gorgeous and you don't even realise. And how that lot are destroying your self-esteem. *That* makes my blood boil.' He hugged me tighter. 'And how I know there's nothing remotely dodgy about the way I feel about you, but that unfortunately other people won't see it that way.'

'What do you mean?' I said.

'You're a student, I'm your teacher. End of.' He sighed again. 'Anyway, come on; we need to get you back to the dorm.'

We walked back together, hand in hand, until we got close to the college. I could tell it was on his mind, the whole teacher/pupil thing, lurking underneath, even while we were chatting. But I'm sixteen and he'll be leaving for a new job soon. We've just got to be cautious for a few weeks. It's not the big deal he's making out.

And here I am, last night of this magical, amazing, life-changing trip, sitting in the bathroom. Still having to pinch myself at what he said. Still feeling what it was like to be in his arms.

Cue orchestra striking up, cue confetti love hearts raining down, cue heavenly choir of cupids singing LARA TITLISS LOVES BEN JAGGER!

MAY 21ST

I am a top-grade, gold-star IMBECILE.

Typical Lara T, I have ballsed up *again* tonight. Filtering thoughts before letting them out of gob? Nah, not me.

Idiot.

Since we got back from the trip, he must've texted me a hundred times and we've talked at pretty much every opportunity on the phone. And there is absolutely not a single second where he is not occupying my mind. Can't eat, sleep, breathe properly. Can't do anything apart from think about him.

The problem is seeing each other without anyone finding out. Obviously, we have to be secret-agent careful at school so no one suspects that I LOVE BEN JAGGER, meaning it's totally *verboten* to talk there. Gran-visiting and karate are the two best meeting-up cover-ups and maybe I'll be hitting the library in town over the next few weeks, to read my A level texts too. *Not.*

Also spending a disproportionate amount of the time I should be devoting to helping Mum, daydreaming about when his contract is up and we can finally come out.

Picturing everyone's face (and by everyone, I mean the triad of girl-evil) for the Big Reveal has become a bit of an obsession actually. When I see Molly's jaw hit the floor, it's going to be priceless. The man she has lusted after all year and he's with me, Loser Lara.

In. Your. Face, Hardy-Jones!

Told Mum I was going to Gran's last night and I did, for ten guilt-ridden minutes, listening for Ben's car pulling up outside the whole while. We drove round for a bit then parked by the reservoir. It was a perfect spring evening, peaceful and warm with birds swooping and chirping the soundtrack to our personal love story. Ben took a picnic blanket from the boot and we walked, arms round each other, into the woods, stopping when we found a grassy clearing, to lie down and watch the stars start to come out. Him stroking my hair, me trying to keep the crazed madwoman grin off my face.

'I can't believe this is happening.' He propped himself up on his elbow. 'You know, if anyone had said I'd end up falling for one of my students, I'd have laughed. No way I'd ever do that in a million years. Not me. And yet here I am.'

'Well, *I'm* glad you did.'

'Me too. Doesn't matter where or when I met you, I know I'd have felt the same. But we can't get away from it: I *am* your teacher and so us being together like this is seriously wrong.' He flopped on to his back. 'I know I should stop right now. In fact, I know the right thing would be to have never started in the first place, but the way I feel about you – I can't *not* see you.'

I shrugged, trying to act nonchalant while inside I was freaking out: *stop right now?* 'But it doesn't matter. Mrs Gill will be back in the autumn. And I could always leave, go to a different school or apply for college. I mean, it's not that I'm even happy at this one, is it? And I'm *sixteen*, not six. Way old enough to know my own mind.'

He took my hand. 'Maybe we shouldn't see each other until my contract's finished. It's too risky.' He stood up and pulled me to my feet.

An invisible hand grabbed at my insides. 'But no one will find out. And if they do, so what?'

'Oh, Lara,' he said sadly. 'I know the way I feel about you is the real thing, but suppose one of your friends goes to Mrs Ellis? Or your mum? What would they think?'

'But I haven't told anyone, I swear.' Panic crept into my voice.

'You know they wouldn't understand.'

'But I want this, I want *you*. And I won't say a word to anyone. I swear on my life.' I was nearly in tears now.

He kissed me on the cheek. 'Come on, let's not spoil a perfect evening.' Then he picked up the picnic blanket and shook off the stray leaves that were clinging to it.

But I couldn't let it go. 'I'm here because I want to be with you, and if anyone says any different, I can tell them that.'

He sighed. 'But that's not how your parents or the school or the police would see things. I'm risking my career – everything – for us to be together. You have to absolutely promise you won't tell a soul.'

'I promise,' I said and he kissed me properly. Then we walked back to the car, me on Bambi legs.

He pulled the car up around the corner so no one

would see us together and we kissed again. 'You know the way I feel towards you is right, don't you?' he said. He put his hand under my chin and tilted my face up to his. 'I would have felt the same if you were sixteen or a hundred and six.'

'Of course.' And it's true. I know he's older and I know the way twisted people might want to read what we have. But there's nothing creepy or wrong. Why would it be so hard to believe that he genuinely cares about me?

Then he said, 'And by the way, I bought you a late birthday present.'

I stared at the box in his hand, astonished, then hurled myself at him, plastering kisses all over his face. 'A new iPod! Oh my God! Thank you, Ben. Thank you thank you thank you!' I screeched.

'So you like it then?' he said, grinning, when I finally let him go.

'Oh, Ben. Are you sure? Thank you so much, it's the best present ever.'

Then impulsively, because I am a fool, I messed everything up.

'I love it. I love *you*.'

My words hung in the air between us until he said,

'Well, I'm pleased you like it. Now go on in, before your mum sends a search party out.'

He gave me a quick peck on the cheek and I got out.

He didn't say it back because he clearly thinks I'm some ditzy, silly girl who sprinkles the L-word like confetti. Even a new iPod isn't worth that.

Idiot.

Later . . . Mum has just been up to my room to give me a hug and (unknowingly) crank up the guilt-o-meter.

'You're such a good girl for spending so long at your gran's again. She gets that lonely stuck in the house on her own and by the time I've finished work and sorted Simon out, I'm too shattered to go round myself.'

So now I feel like a fool AND a fraudster. Must stick around at Gran's tomorrow for more than just a hello/goodbye fly-past.

Oh God, what is he going to think of me blurting it out like that?

I may *die* of cringe.

11.23 A text: *Listen to number 7 xx* Worked out what he meant: he's put a playlist on the iPod. Switched it straight on: beautiful, melancholy piano and vocals about giving up on love then finding the right person.

Ten minutes later, another text: *I love you too. x*
Squeeeeeaaaal!

MAY 22ND

He loves me! He loves me! He loves me!

I love him and he loves me and nothing else in the whole world matters. Met up again tonight. I told Mum I was off to karate (guilt guilt guilt – missed two weeks now) and we ended up driving to the nature park again. Well, not like we can pop to Costa for a cappuccino, is it?

'I want to show you off,' he said. 'My family and friends will love you. I hate skulking about like we're doing something wrong.' Pause. 'Well, I mean, I know technically we *are* doing something wrong, but it doesn't feel like that to me.'

I snuggled up closer, wallowing in the feel of him. 'I want to be with you more than anything else in the world. Not as if you've got a gun to my head, is it?'

'You and me know that. Other people won't.'

'OK, so let's meet at your house, then we can spend more time together and no one will find out.'

I resigned myself to another round of 'Reasons that's

not a good idea' and he duly obliged. Key features of this discussion include 'not wanting to take advantage' and 'not rush into anything'. Both of these evidently euphemisms for 'not creating an opportunity to have sex'. Like having sex with him would be something bad?! I mean, I know we'd be moving into very big, very serious new territory, but bluntly, I AM GAGGING FOR IT.

I must be the only virgin left in Year 11. And it's not like I'd be chucking my cherry away round the back of the sports hall with some loser from the boys' school (à la Molly Hardy-Jones). Ben is the love of my life and I know I will NEVER feel this way about anyone but him.

MAY 23RD

Amber guilt-flood alert in force.

Ben trusted me to keep our Top Secret zipped, but Emma rang to ask how Cambridge went tonight and, well, the truth just kind of slipped out. Couldn't help it. Didn't mean to.

'Awesome, I had the best time ever,' I told her, virtually purring the cat-that-got-the-cream note in my voice.

'Aw, that's great,' she said. 'You really deserve something good at the moment.'

Told her about meeting Minty, Satty and Fanny; how we're staying in touch on Facebook and about the lectures making my mind up about doing English at uni.

'And Sir Sex-on-Legs?' she asked, 'How was he?'

'You mean Ben . . .' I said.

She laughed. 'Oh right, "Ben" now is it? Veerry cosy.'

I think it was the way she laughed, almost making fun of me. Or maybe I literally could not hold it in any longer. Anyway, whatever: I told her.

Ooops.

She went very, very quiet and when she finally spoke her voice had completely changed. 'Please tell me you're joking, Lara.'

'I'm not, it's true,' I said happily. 'I can't believe it either. Sir Sex-on-Legs and me! He picked me!'

But Emma was definitely not joining me in getting giddy with it. In fact, she was acting like I'd informed her I had days to live. 'Tell me I'm not hearing this right.'

'You are.'

'He kissed you.'

'Yes.'

'And now you're seeing him, your *teacher*?'

'Yes, well, no. He's my *boyfriend*. He won't be my teacher for much longer.'

This time, the line was silent for so long I thought she'd hung up. 'Em?'

'I'm still here, I just don't know what to say. I mean, isn't it *illegal*?'

'How about saying you're pleased I'm happy for once?' I said, echoing her frosty tone, 'Or glad I've met someone?'

'Come on,' she said, 'you know I want you to be happy, I just don't think this is the way. I mean, have you thought this through? We're talking about a man, a *teacher*, for God's sake. Not some sixth former from the boys' school.'

From downstairs, I heard the key turn in the front door. 'Look, Mum's just got in. I'd better go. SWEAR you won't breathe a word.'

'If you don't want me to tell anyone, I won't,' she said, with obvious reluctance. 'But you are headed for disaster on this one, Lara, trust me.'

'I'm home!' called Mum as she stepped into the hall.

'Gotta go,' I said.

'Think about what I said,' Emma replied, 'Ring you tomorrow.'

'OK, bye.'

Don't think I'll tell Ben, he'll only get worked up about it. Plus, he doesn't need to know I broke the only promise he's ever asked me to keep.

It'll be all right. If I can trust anyone, it's Emma.

MAY 24TH

Me and Simon met up with Dad at McDonald's. (The man has no imagination. How about pizza once in a while?)

'I've got some news,' he said. 'I've decided I'm going to stay with your Uncle Andy for a while. He's more orders than he can handle so I'd be doing him a favour.' He stared down at his coffee. 'And I could do with some time away to sort myself out.'

Translating from the adultspeak, I interpreted this as, *Stop drinking and try to win back your mother.*

'But I'll come back every other weekend to see you both, and you can come down in the holidays. You'd like that, spending some time with Emma.'

'Yeah, definitely,' I said. (Although what came after changed my mind about *that*.)

'And I'm sorry for everything that's happened

recently. Things have just sort of . . . sort of . . . got on top of me for a while and I'm so ashamed.' He swallowed hard. 'I l-love your mum and you two more than anything. I hate myself for letting you down.'

Simon's lip trembled. 'It's not fair, Daddy! Uncle Andy's miles away. I want you back home with me and Paddington.'

'Oh, little man,' Dad said, kissing him on the forehead. 'I don't want to go either. I want to see you all the time, but it's the way that things have to be, until me and your mum get back on track and we can be like we were before. A proper family.'

Well, that tipped me over into boohooing like a baby too, and while the three of us sat there bawling away in McDonald's, the stone of anger I've been carrying inside since the Bed Incident crumbled to dust. Dad's words lit a tiny spark of hope that maybe things could be all right again. I don't think Simon gets it though. The little fella's been blubbering ever since.

Sent Ben a text as soon as I could: *Think I've sorted it out with my dad.* x

Got one straight back, *I'm really glad. I love you so much.* x

Yes!!!

Might forward it on to Emma later, as evidence.

Came close to properly falling out with her tonight for the first time ever. I honestly thought she'd be on my side, excited even. I mean, she's seen his picture, I've told her how I'd have been in pieces without him, but she's reacting like he's some kind of paedo.

'You have to tell him you can't see him again. Not out of school,' she said, in her big I'm-a-serious-grown-up voice.

Who put you in charge? I thought.

'No way!' I said. 'I *love* him, I'm not going to dump him.'

'I know you've got feelings for him,' she said, 'but this is majorly wrong. You must realise you can't go out with one of your teachers!'

'I'm sixteen years old, I think I get to choose who to go out with, thanks.'

'Exactly! You're sixteen; it is actually illegal.'

'Noooo, because sixteen is *actually* the age of consent. And we haven't done it anyway, for your information.' Snippy now, she was getting on my nerves. 'Why are you being like this?'

'Because it IS illegal if he's your teacher, you dumb-ass. It doesn't matter if you're sixteen, seventeen, eighteen as long as he teaches you, it's against the law. I looked it up on the internet. He could go to *prison*.'

Extreme sarkiness. 'Oh well, if it was on the *internet* then it must be true, mustn't it?' Then, nicking a Mum-classic conversation closer, 'I am not getting anything out of this discussion, so I'm going to end it now. Bye'

'La—' came down the line, but I'd already pressed End Call.

Pleased? Happy for me? Jealous? Any of those possible reactions, but negative? I'd never have guessed that. Lara T's trademark yap-trap strikes again. Why did I tell her?

Later . . . Oh God! If Dad moves to Uncle Andy's then Emma's bound to let it slip sooner or later.

Shit.

MAY 25TH

Had top brainwave *re* Emma.

Texted her, *Thought about what you said. Can't believe I was so stupid. Have finished it. Feel daft. Please keep secret xxx*

Haven't had a reply yet, not convinced she's that gullible, but it's worth a try. And you know what, I don't feel even the tiniest bit guilty for it. *Finish with him.* As if!

Can't see him tonight (Year 8 parents' evening), but we managed to snatch a few minutes in his stock cupboard over lunch. Very risky, frisky business, but it's got a lock so we just had to be mute mouse-quiet. We kissed for so long, I had to buy emergency chapstick on the way home. He's wearing my lips away.

Just been reading his horoscope.

Your sexual style fascinates men in June so trust your intuition. Your sixth sense is quivering around a blonde colleague with a cheeky sense of fun. Make square-toed shoes and flirty florals with a nod to vintage your signature style this month.

Hmmmm.

Normal schools let their pupils have a break after the exams. Not ours. That would be too suspiciously like being nice to us and THAT'S the top of a slippery slope. Next thing we'd be demanding study leave, edible food in the canteen, clean toilets, non-tedious teachers, etc. and who knows what anarchy that would cause?

So while every other Year 11 in the country is lying hungover in the back garden on a weekday, we've already started doing the prep for our AS year. (Which assumes we've passed our GCSEs of course.)

Every member of 11G is cursing this stupid rule . . .
Except me.

Later . . . Text from Emma: *Ring me? x*
Haven't answered.

MAY 27TH

We got spotted together tonight, but I'm fairly sure we got away with it. This time. If we carry on sneaking around like this, I won't have a pair of dry pants left soon.

Took Paddington out for a Ben-rendezvous at Greenhead Park, play-acting 'Ooh, fancy meeting you here' in case anyone we knew from school was about. Anyway, the coast was clear (initially) so we headed for a bench screened by some trees, tucked out of sight of the main path.

We were engaged in some in-depth snogging when Ben suddenly broke away. Paddington was yowling in riotous disharmony with another dog off in the trees.

'I'll have to go get her,' I said, heading for the noise.

'Hey, you can't go disappearing off into the woods on your own. It's not safe.'

We tramped through the trees, hand in hand, to find Paddington racing to get away from a yappy little dog/rat frantically twerking round her.

My heart sank. 'Oh God,' I whispered, pulling Ben urgently back. 'Go back to the bench. *Now*. It's Beyoncé.'

'Eh?' he said, but it was too late. Satan's homie, Mr Themnextdoor, had appeared.

I dropped Ben's hand like a hot potato, but we'd been noticed. A sly smile curled somewhere in the folds of his grimy grey beard. 'All right.'

'Hello,' I answered. 'Paddington, come on, girl. Come on.'

After about five increasingly agonised pleas, she deigned to come. 'Stupid idiot dog,' I muttered, slipping her lead on.

'Who's Gandalf?' asked Ben when we'd moved out of earshot.

'Who?'

'Your mate there, Hairy McScary.'

'Oh, evil next-door neighbour.' We were back on the path by now and heading for the car.

Ben stopped, shocked.

'Oh God, really? How likely is he to tell your mum he saw you?'

I honestly don't know the answer to that. Not like he invites her round for coffee, but he might drop me in it just to stir.

'If we met up at your house, this wouldn't happen,' I said, expecting the customary noble speech about Honouring My Maidenly Virtue, etc. But . . .

'You're right; this is getting far too dangerous. OK, what are you up to on Thursday?'

WOW! 'Visiting my granny, I suppose,' I said with a wink.

'Please don't joke about it.' He tapped me on the leg with the end of the lead. 'I hate the fact you're lying to your mum because of me.'

'OK. One: technically, I'm not lying because I will see Gran first. And two: I'm doing it because *I* want to, not because of you.'

He gave me a reproving look and remorse rushed back in.

'I should just resign now. End all this lying.'

Ha! *Hardly the response of a man taking shagvantage, is it, Emma?*

'But you wouldn't get a reference,' I pointed out. 'Plus we need you at school. You're the best teacher we've got. And it's only a few more weeks.'

And what are weeks when we've got the rest of our lives together?

Later . . . Another text from Emma. *I'm around tonight if you want to talk. xx*

Ha! Looks like she's fallen for the sob split story. Still can't forgive her betrayal though. I expected more from her.

June

JUNE 1ST

There's a neon sign flashing I LOVE BEN JAGGER!
above my head with a big arrow pointing straight at him.
When we catch each other's eye across the classroom,
everyone else vanishes; the air crackles like a storm
is brewing and a tsunami-sized *frisson* crashes down.
An orchestra plays, flowers burst into bloom, cute
wildlife scampers into view and the room is a fairy-tale
Disney glade.

So how come no one else at school has even
noticed?!

Honestly, he could tap-dance naked on the desk,

singing 'I love La-ra I love La-ra' to the tune of 'La Cucaracha' and the rest of the class would carry on doing their stupid work and asking their dumb questions.

How can they be so *blind*?

Grrrr. He's busy tonight playing five-a-side. To see him all day and not be able to talk to him is torture enough, but then not to see him later. UnBEARable.

Got another log to chuck on the Fire of Guilt. (Although towering inferno might be a more accurate metaphor.) Keep having little panics about the exams. Mum was going on today about booking a restaurant so we can celebrate on Results Day.

I couldn't think about anything but him the whole time; even when I got my books out for some hardcore studying, within seconds I was doodling his face in my notebook or writing *Lara Jagger* over everything. Obsessed doesn't begin to cover it. But how can I tell her there'll be nothing to celebrate?

Mum's going to be so disappointed in me. Zombifying long hours (to pay *my* school fees) and the only thing I can do is count down the minutes till I can sneak round to Ben's house tomorrow. She needs me more than ever now Dad's gone and I'm not even really here. I'm lying left, right and centre while my whole family is falling apart.

And the Award for World's Worst Daughter goes to . . .

JUNE 2ND

It was sooo funny in registration today. Molly made some bitchy comment about me. I didn't actually hear it, but Ben did and I could see he was fighting not to rip her to shreds.

'You need to spend more time on your personality and less on your appearance, Molly.'

God, she was so pissed off!

Emma rang tonight, giving it Mrs Sympathy and niceness with her 'tough decision' and 'right choice' noises. She has completely swallowed the fictional break-up sob story and to keep my cover I had to pretend to go along with it, throwing in the odd wistful sniff for authenticity, when all the time I was thinking: Ha, stick it, Sister! Me and Mr J are *dandy*.

'It's just so hard,' I whispered in a suitably downtrodden voice.

'I know,' she said, 'but I am so glad you've done it. I was really worried.'

OK, so I get her motives are genuine and she doesn't want to see me hurt. Yes. Get that loud and clear. Buuuut if she really understood me, she'd be cheerleading for Team Ben/Lara. Without him, my life would comprise poverty, bullying and separated parents. Nothing and no one is going to stop me having him.

JUNE 3RD

Flicked through Mum's back issues of *Cosmopolitan* tonight, hoping to pick up some useful tips, but have reached the conclusion that sex is something you just have to get on with, like swimming. Dive in and hope your limbs act on instinct maybe?

My grasp of the theory is excellent. I totally get the mechanics. Now desperate to back it up with some practical experience.

No idea how much to 'mow my lady lawn' and obsessing about it. Mum doesn't keep a machete handy so made do with a spot of nail-scissor topiary. Not perfect, but at least he won't bounce straight off now. Shaved my legs and scrubbed myself to a nice shade of radioactive lobster. Larded on so much of mum's posh body lotion I look like I'm about to swim the channel.

Oh my God, somebody pinch me. All this is because tomorrow I am finally going to DO IT with BEN JAGGER.

Last thing and it's a weird one. Mikaela ran in and tried to take a photo of me in the shower after PE, but I snatched up my towel in time. Yawn. I am so over their stupid, childish antics. What is it with all the photos?

Are you a *lesbian*, Mikaela?

Sorry, I'm spoken for.

Later . . . Just got a text: *I miss you xxx*. I love him so much it hurts. Actual physical hurty hurt, like toothache. (Although nicer.)

Can't sleep for thinking about tomorrow. Bit nervous am going to do something wrong, but mainly over-the-galaxy happy that I will get to share the most special moment of my life with him.

Waaah!

JUNE 4TH

A* English student I may be, but even I don't have the vocabulary to describe how incredible . . . amazing . . . fantastic . . . and mind-blowing it . . . wasn't.

Yep. *Wasn't.*

Got there, had a cup of tea and watched *Into theWild.* (Great film.) After the credits rolled we talked, had a kiss . . . Then just when I was thinking, *Here we go! Time to hop on board the Friskytown Express*, he went, 'Right, let's get you home then,' and with that verbal bucket of cold water, jumped off the sofa.

'I don't want to go home,' I said. 'I want to *be* with you. Properly.'

He didn't miss my meaning and sat back down. 'We can't. It's not that I don't want to. God, Lara, it's driving me mad. You're so beautiful, I fancy you more than anyone on the planet. But you're too young.'

'Too young? I'm sixteen. Plus I'm the only girl in my whole year who hasn't done it.'

'I sincerely doubt that,' he said with a smile. 'Look, when I think of you, I picture an amazing girl I've fallen in love with. I never think of you as a pupil and when I do, it makes me feel like a perv. I don't want what we have to be sleazy and wrong.'

'I'm sixteen,' I said again, sliding my hand under his T-shirt, 'which is exactly why it isn't sleazy and it isn't wrong.'

He gently extracted my hand and held my wrists

on my knees. 'Your age is irrelevant because I'm your *teacher*. Anything we do outside school is wrong.'

'No one would know,' I persisted, moving my hands up around his neck. 'I love you and I want to be a proper girlfriend. I won't go shooting my mouth off, you know.'

That was his cue to stand up. 'Believe me, there is nothing I want more either and I know I can trust you. But no.'

And that was that. All that effort for nothing.

I've had such a bad day (Mum in a mood, Molly in bitch overdrive) that the thought of tonight with him was the only thing keeping me sane. Oh, I don't know, what should I have done, pounced on him? I wouldn't have the guts in a million years.

And so my Maidenly Virtue remains intact and I'm left thinking, *He says he loves me, but does he fancy me too?*

Seriously think I've had racier nights watching Noel Edmonds with Gran.

JUNE 5TH

I was pissed off enough last night at still being a virgin. Now I am even more pissed off because Sam Short tried to SET MY HAIR ON FIRE.

Had to get the bus again as weather Armageddon arrived, complete with leaden skies, high winds and bucketing rain. As soon as the doors opened, I saw that lot grinning and froze, one foot on, one foot off. Charming Mr Driver grumped, 'What you waiting for, Red, a written invitation?' and folded me up in the door. My satchel strap got trapped and the driver, working overtime to bag himself a place in the Dickhead Hall of Fame, pretended he hadn't noticed.

'Hey, Titless,' said Sam, 'you been avoiding me or what?'

As usual I tried to ignore him, but couldn't get away as my bag had me stuck fast. Don't dare risk the Ben iPod at school, so forced to listen. Sam lifted up a lock of my newly-dyed hair, tutting.

'What was the point of doing that, Titless? You can't polish shit, you know.'

Ben's words echoed in my head. *Stand up to them. Don't let yourself be a pushover, Lara.*

'Get your hands off me, you midget,' I said.

OK, hardly *Take a bow, Oscar Wilde*, I know, but I *was* trapped in an automatic door. Some of the kids laughed as the floorshow began and Molly came barging up, knocking Year 7s down like dominoes.

'You take that back. You can't call him names.'

In one quick movement, Sam drew a lighter from his blazer pocket and held it to the lock of my hair, thumb poised to flick it into life.

'One more word, you ginger cow, and I *will* do it.'

I tried to pull my head back, desperately hoping the driver might intervene, but he'd developed a terminal case of the oblivions, the ignorant twat.

Sam pulled even harder. 'You have no idea how much I want to do this.' His eyes were bright with fury. 'Call me that again. Go on, I dare you.'

My mouth went for it before my brain had even registered the challenge.

'Midget.'

Click. There was a crackle followed by a *whumpf* and an instant acrid reek. I flung my hands up, but luckily only the bit he'd been holding had frazzled.

'Oy!' shouted the driver, senses miraculously restored. 'No smoking on the bus.'

Sam grinned, replacing the lighter in his blazer pocket. 'Sorry, mate.' Then he turned back to me. 'Next time it won't just be your hair, Titless. You need to learn to keep that . . .' he swiped his hand across my mouth '. . . *shut*.'

I couldn't let him see I was bothered, so I marched off when we stopped, but inside I was trembling. My first instinct was to run and tell Ben, but how can I? He'll go mad, *really* mad, and I can't let people put two and two together.

JUNE 7TH

Went round to Ben's house earlier. At about half nine, he gave me and my Maidenly Virtue a lift back home, despite my very best efforts to leave it behind on the sofa.

Can't commit the details to paper as I have already cringed so far up my own bottom that I'll be brushing my teeth by torchlight tonight. Suffice it to say there was a tragic amateur seduction attempt (me) followed by a kind and noble speech about 'not taking advantage' (him).

My mind was dying of embarrassment while my body was screaming *take advantage!* Anyway, he switched the subject to school, so I related heavily edited lowlights of how the bullying has gone up a notch (glossing over psycho Sam and the lighter). Said it was name-calling, nothing physical, and he treated me to another of his, 'Arise, oppressed woman, and overthrow the shackles, etc. etc.' speeches. He never stops nagging me about it.

'You need to tell your mum what's going on so she can speak to Molly's parents.' I shut him up with a snog. But I love the fact he cares, even if I have completely forbidden him from intervening. I can put up with it. It's only a few weeks more.

And yay! All hail Mother Nature for a beautiful non-rainy day which spared me the Hellbus today.

Rang Dad before I went out. He sounds a ton happier than he has recently. Unsurprisingly, working with Uncle Andy is much more his cup of tea than rotting in the 'grotty bedsit'. Also, a cup of tea is the strongest drink he's had since he left, so he claims. He was quite chipper, almost his old self. Mum smiled when I told her which was a bit freaky tbh (it's been a while).

Then her expression changed and she frowned. 'I meant to say before, the man from next door said something very weird to me this morning.'

I managed to croak out a convincingly uninterested, 'Really?'

'Mmmm, yes. The gist of it was he'd seen you up to no good in the woods with a boy. But I know he must have got his wires crossed. You haven't been seeing anyone, have you?'

'I wish,' I sighed, melodramatically placing my hands over my heart and Mum laughed.

'Thought so. He's proper . . .' and she whistled and mimed *cuckoo*. 'All those drugs and whatnot have fried his brains.'

I laughed too, mainly from relief, it has to be said. BUT . . . so you'd have to be mentally ill to believe I could get a boyfriend, eh, Mum?

Cheers.

JUNE 9TH

Narrowly escaped another potential attack after school. Rumour has it Molly thinks I had a hand in her losing the talent show. Yeah, right. With a voice like that, she didn't need anyone's help. I wasn't even a judge, it was the staff. Paranoid bint.

Spotted Mikaela and Jabba the Flett lurking by the bike rack. Molly was there too, sucking on Sam's face like a drowning woman who's found a snorkel. *Spew.* The pair of them are so gross.

I was deliberating fight or flight when Ben walked

past and they legged it. He didn't see me either, but knowing he was there gave me the warm 'n' fuzzies. And of course it meant I could hop on my bike and pedal away, safe and sound. Officially, I was at Gran's for the evening, but I didn't even wait for the kettle to boil, just slung the shopping on the worktop, gave her a quick peck on the cheek and dashed down to Ben's car. *Guilt guilt guilt.*

Then after we'd been at his for an hour or so, something very unexpected happened. Nothing to do with my Maidenly Virtue (if only, eh?). No, we were snuggled up on the sofa watching telly and chatting, when *bbrrinnng!!!* I nearly leapt out of my skin. We looked at each other, shock mirrored in our faces.

'You'd better go through to the kitchen,' he said. 'Just in case.'

I knelt down under the window and peeped through the slats in the blind.

Grumpy Cow Secretary in fifty layers of slap and an orange bodycon dress. I was too far away to make out the words, but I could see her, bobbing on the lawn like a spacehopper.

Ben's voice came floating back down the hall. 'No, Dawn, you can't.'

I almost sprained my ears trying to catch her response, but *mumble mumble*.

'That's none of your business!' he said indignantly.

Insanely desperate to know what they were arguing about, did I dare to try to open the window?

YES!

Slowly, slowly, I cranked the handle, inching it up while Ben's voice grew increasingly irate and her gestures more frantic. Slowly, slowly, I nudged the window open, tiny push by tiny push – until it suddenly sprang open with a loud *creeeaaak!*

She whipped round like someone had just shouted, *Free pies!*

'Have you got a woman in there?'

'What? No.'

'There is! Someone's just opened that window. So that's why you dumped me then, you two-timing bastard.'

'Dawn, please will you go. I'm sorry you feel badly done by, but I need you to leave.'

I could almost see her brain ticking off the options: *1. Angry. 2. Pleading.* 'But babe, you KNOW we could make it work if you gave me another chance.'

He looked disgusted. 'Huh! Even if I wanted to,

which I don't, I don't see how after what you said to my sister.'

'God,' she said (trying out *3. Defensive*). 'I can't believe you're dragging that up. I told you, I had too much to drink. No biggie.'

'Dawn, you trashed her in front of two hundred people.'

'You know I didn't mean it.'

'You called her "an obese pig in a cheap dress" . . .'

'It was a JOKE.'

'. . . at her *wedding reception*.'

'All right, I'll tell her I'm sorry if you want,' she said.

He carried on as if she hadn't spoken. 'She had to edit the best man's speech out of the video because of you. My family would disown me if we got back together and, frankly, you're nowhere *near* worth the hassle.'

Ouch!

'Well, I hated your stupid family anyway,' she sneered. 'They are so up themselves. No wonder your sister's got no sense of humour.'

'Just go, will you?' He started to close the door, then paused. 'Actually, while you're here, you may as well give me my keys back.'

'I haven't got them on me, you'll have to wait,' she

tossed the words back over her shoulder as she stomped back to her car.

He called after her, 'Well, I want them back, otherwise I'm going to have to change the locks and it'll cost me a fortune.'

But she didn't reply and instead turned square on to the kitchen window, shouting, 'You're welcome to him, whoever you are!'

He was giving off *I don't want to talk about it* vibes loud and clear when he came back in, but I couldn't resist prodding. 'How did you meet her?'

He shrugged. 'She's my mate's girlfriend's cousin and when I moved up here I didn't know that many people.' Then he went on about how when they were an item she was always moaning at him. 'Apparently I made her unhappy and I was a rubbish boyfriend.'

Rubbish boyfriend??! Is she completely insane?

'But you must've been OK together at first,' I insisted.

'Yeah, I suppose, she was a laugh at first. I was a bit lonely too. And I owed her a lot for telling my mate about the job at school, so I kind of fell into it really. Three months of my life I'd rather forget. Anyway, then she ruined my sister's wedding and that was the last straw. Now all I want is my keys back and she's playing silly buggers.' He turned his head so he was looking in my eyes. 'Do you think I'm a rubbish boyfriend too?'

'Course not,' I said and gave him a kiss while New Year fireworks exploded in my heart.

Boyfriend!!!

JUNE 12TH

Seen him nearly every day this week. The Gran Guilt is now cranked up to oh-no-she's-gonna-blow level AND they rang to see why I'd not been to karate. Had to lie and say I'd hurt my back. Then they sent me a sweet Get Well card, which (ironically) gave me a coronary when I opened it with Mum in the room. Luckily, she didn't twig what it was.

Cannot WAIT until his contract ends.

When I'm not with him, time goes into slo-mo and I swear the clocks power dow-dow-dowwwwwn, then speed back up when I *am* with him so everything goes double-quick time and, before I know it, it's time to go back home and I feel like I have had about a second with him, which is no time at all because I want to say so much to him and do so much with him. Waaaaah!!!

There isn't enough *time*.

V. v. annoyed he keeps switching his phone off because Dawn (aka Grumpy Cow Secretary) is stalking him. I don't *think* she's been round again since the other night. (He would have told me, wouldn't he?)

He is absolutely seething about the keys. Got a quote from a locksmith and it's going to cost nearly £300!! So he said he's going to have to wait till payday to get it done. Yes! His last payday before he finishes and we can stop all this sneaking around.

Dawn Longbottom aka Grumpy Cow: you had him, you blew it. Move on.

I have never felt this happy in my whole life. I am literally a bliss grenade, pin popped and primed to explode.

JUNE 13TH

Since the end of Year 9, I've had this Pavlovian response to blonde hair extensions and fake tan. Even from a distance, my whole body instantly flips to quivering bunny-scents-prowling-fox mode.

Sam, Mikaela, Chloe, Fat Graham Flett, I know they've all had a part to play as well, but she's the Big

Boss. Molly Hardy-Jones has made me a nervous wreck: she's taken all my friends away; made me feel ugly and worthless; humiliated me in public; physically and verbally abused me; destroyed my possessions; slagged off my family and threatened my mum.

BUT things are changing. Not her, she's evil incarnate, but me. I can't change what *she* thinks about me, but I can change what *I* think about me.

Meeting the girls at Cambridge proves I can make friends who are fabulous. And every mirror tells me I am *not* the ugliest of them all. Dad's working again, Mum's doing OK. And, most of all, Ben Jagger LOVES me.

Put it together and what have you got?

Molly is so full of shit.

My epiphany.

So back to today. Thanks to her, I've been suffering wee-related torment for weeks, but lunchtime today, it was brave the toilets or have my kidneys implode. No sooner had I gone in than she was there.

'Got something to tell you, Titless.'

'Give it a rest,' I said, pushing open a cubicle door.

She slammed it shut in front of me. 'I've got a message from Sam. He says you can't hide from him forever.'

Suddenly, I felt so very, very tired of all of her

ridiculous, melodramatic threats. Revenge, messages, punishment threats from very low-budget Mafia moll Molly.

Whatever.

'OK then, give him a message from me. Tell him I said to go fu–' the main door opened and a Year 7 girl walked in, eyeing us warily '–ck himself.'

'Get out!' Molly snarled and the poor girl scuttled off.

'Don't you get *bored* of being a bitch, Molly?' I said when we were on our own again.

She glared at me. 'Just passing on a message.'

'And Sam as well. I mean, he doesn't even know me,' I replied to her departing back. 'Why is he bothered?'

She hesitated, then turned slowly back round to face me.

'He hates you, Titless. Like I hate you. You think you're Lady Einstein and everyone else is thick. Making out my boyfriend's a joke, calling him stupid names. But *you're* the joke. Even Chloe can't stand you. And your tragic crush on Mr Jagger is pathetic.'

My heart began to pound. *Had she seen us?*

'He totally ignores you and you still do it. You've really got no self-respect at all, have you?'

And that's when I had my *Ping!* Light-bulb moment.

Ben ignores me, does he?

I swear I do not know how I held back from lashing her with the truth. But I managed to bite my tongue, thank God. Not that she'd have believed me anyway.

So if she's wrong about all of that, then she's wrong about everything.

Epiphany.

JUNE 14TH

'Celebrated' Simon's birthday today with possibly the gloomiest party ever.

The three of us ate pizza and watched a DVD. Mum had made a chocolate cake with a 7 in Smarties on the top, but Simon majorly sulked because Dad wasn't there to blow out the candles with him. In the end, Mum got so annoyed with his whining that she sent him off to bed. Then (predictably) she felt mean, came upstairs and I can hear them both crying together in Simon's room now. And because it was 'family time', I didn't even get to sneak out to see Ben.

Bah.

But that's OK because only a few weeks and I'll

be a sixth former with a gorgeous boyfriend who just happens to be a teacher. A teacher in *another school*. Expecting some raised eyebrows at first, but it won't last once everyone sees us and recognises we're meant to be together. There'll be a newer, juicier scandal along a week later and we'll be left in peace. And Molly and that lot won't dare get within a million miles of me once they know.

Life-of-my-dreams is about to come true!

It's going to be amazing and incredible and fabulous and fantastic! I'll get to see him whenever I want and no one will be able to stop us. We'll be free to go to the pictures and for a coffee and anywhere we want. My happy-ever-after is just around the corner.

I CANNOT WAIT!!!!!!!!!!

JUNE 15TH

Oh God.

Everything's fallen apart.

He isn't answering his phone. I need to speak to him more than anything and it puts me straight to voicemail. Writing in here now because I literally haven't got a clue what else to do.

ANSWER THE PHONE, BEN!

It's all my fault. I should never have gone along with his 'Stand up to them and they'll back down' bollocks. This is Huddersfield, not Hollywood. You can't wave a mascara wand and *abracadabra* Lara's the Prom Princess. Stupid stupid stupid. And now I need to speak to him; I need to know what's happening.

What has he done? Where is he? Why won't he pick up?

I'll write down what I know so far, see if I can get things straight in my head.

The class was waiting for English to start. Break had finished, but Ben hadn't come in yet. An opportunity for Molly to sharpen her claws.

'Can anyone else smell shit?' she asked no one in particular. 'Actually, it's more like . . . ooooh, what is it? Pigs! That's it, pig.'

She came over to my desk where I was reading, minding my own business. 'It's really strong round here. Hang on, not pig, dog, that's it. Dog shit.' She did a mock double take. 'Wait a minute. Titless, you're a dog and your mum cleans up other people's shit. Yep, it's coming fr–'

I jumped up so quickly she stumbled backwards.

'What IS your problem?'

The room fell quiet.

'Go on. Tell me why you can't grow up and LEAVE.
ME. ALONE.'

I shouted the last three words. Everyone else was
now transfixed by the spectacle of me, Loser Lara,
confronting the Queen of Mean.

'*You're* my problem, Titless. Your ugly face and the
way –'

I didn't let her finish. '*My* ugly face? I AM NOT UGLY.
Have you got that? *You're* the ugly one. Inside and out,
through and through. Ugly, ugly, ugly.' She thrust her face
up so close I could see every foundation-crusted pore.

'I'm not ugly. You take that back, you no-tit freak.'

'No chance. *If you can't take it, don't say it*, isn't that
what you told me? And as for having no tits, yeah, it's
true, I am flat-chested. But so what? I've got a good
brain. Whereas you –' I waved between her boobs and
her head '– have a big saggy pair and no . . . Well, do you
see the correlation?'

She glared at me, a dark red flush creeping up
her neck.

'Sorry, Molly. Correlation's a big word. I mean *link*.
Do you see the link?'

'Shut your mouth. You're a loser and everyone knows it.' She almost spat the words at me.

'You know what? I am *so* bored of you and the lame bollocks you say over and over. Is that the best you can do? *No tits, no friends, ginger, loser blah blah blah.*'

I drew in a deep breath to continue my apocalyptic rant. 'And I can speak to you however I want. You and your boyfriend and your little tribe of hangers-on. Your boyfriend. Ha! He treats you like dirt and you're too thick to see it. Or desperate, I don't know. And your so-called friends don't even like you, you've just bullied them into being in your little gang to make you feel a bit better about yourself.'

Stuff I'd been saying to her in my head for ages came pouring out of my mouth in this unstoppable monologue. Some part of my brain registered the other girls, but they were like the audience for a play. As far as I was concerned, it was just me and Molly in the classroom, face to face for the dramatic climactic scene.

I sighed theatrically. 'You know, if I thought you actually deserved one iota of sympathy, I think I might almost feel sorry for you.'

There was a long pause, then she smirked. 'You finished, Titless?' and opened her iPad case. '*I've* got no friends, have I? Well, let's check out what the world thinks of *you*.'

She held the computer in front of me and there it was on the screen. A Facebook page with bold letters blaring across the top: ***Lara Titless Deserves to Die*** Above it icons showing twenty-eight smiling, happy 'friends'.

Words jumped out. 'Ugly' 'ginger' 'bitch' 'show-off' 'freak'. Molly tapped on the photo icon revealing 'Competition Entries' and those random phone pictures from the past few months flashed up: me on the toilet, being spat on, drenched in Coke, hair being set alight and, of course, me with my bra wrenched up, everything on show. Every single one was captioned with votes and comments.

'LMFAO!!!'

'Ginger minger.'

'I hate her'

'Burn the ugly bitch!'

It was like I'd been punched in the guts.

Molly's voice was loud now. 'So don't you talk to me about how *I've* got no friends when this is what people think of you, Titless. Everyone hates you, not just me and my "hangers-on". Everyone. All these comments, all these people reading the messages.

Look, we've even got you a YouTube channel'

And she danced her fingers across the screen until the page transformed into a sea of video icons with titles like 'Titless Titliss'. I turned my head, not wanting to see the details, but she shoved it right in my face. I managed to bat it away, but not before I registered 221 hits.

On 221 occasions people have thought it was funny to look at videos of me being tortured and humiliated? 221 times I've been stripped topless in the street? On the toilet? Spat on?

I felt on the verge of throwing up. Paralysed. Couldn't move, couldn't say a word. Molly's triumph was written all over her face and she was almost panting with malicious excitement. The class was mesmerised and silenced by us squaring up, two boxers in the ring.

Then . . .

. . . Ben walked in.

'Sorry I'm late, ladies. Meeting overran.' He stopped. His eye passed from my horrified expression to the iPad Molly was holding.

'Lara, what is it? What's going on?'

I couldn't answer. Ben plucked the iPad from Molly's hands and she lunged after it.

'That's mine Sir!' but it was already out of reach.

'Please don't look,' I said quietly.

Too late. There was an agonising silence while he frowned at the screen, Molly and I twin statues on either side.

'Let me get this straight, Molly,' he said eventually. 'You have set up a Facebook page calling for the death of one of your classmates.'

Another futile grab. 'Sir. It wasn't me. I didn't start it, I swear.'

Ignoring her completely, he continued. 'There's a Facebook page here saying one of your classmates should die and —' he tapped the screen '— a series of videos, posted in the public domain.'

'But, Sir —'

'Shut up and sit down,' he said without looking up, voice still calm. 'Lara, did you know about this?'

'Not till now,' I said miserably. 'Please don't look at any more.'

'No, of course not. I've seen all I need to.'

Molly held out her hand as he closed the case. He looked at her with total repugnance. 'You have got to be kidding. You're not getting this back until Mrs Ellis has seen what you've been up to.'

'I didn't do it. Well, not all of it,' she said, eyes

wide. 'Honest, Sir. It was Sam's idea.'

'Sam? Who's Sam?'

'Sam Short, Sir. At the boys' school.'

'Ah. Sam Short. Your boyfriend, isn't he?'

'Yes, Sir,' she mumbled, looking down at the floor. 'Sort of.'

'And he set all this up, told people about it?'

'Yes. Facebook, YouTube, the texting . . . everything.'

'Texting?'

She carried on staring at the floor. 'Titless, I mean *Lara's* mum gave me her number and I gave it to Sam. He was texting her.'

That was a surprise. So Sam was the phantom phone menace, not Molly.

'I see. And this "competition". What's that all about?'

'The best picture.'

'Right. Let me get this straight before I go to Mrs Ellis,' Ben said. 'Sam Short harassed Lara with threatening texts? He encouraged you and your friends to put Lara in embarrassing or upsetting situations so they could *take photos* of her? And *film* her?'

'Yes, Sir.'

'Which your boyfriend would then post on the internet so that . . .?'

'People could vote on the best one, Sir. But it's not all Sam's fault. She asked for it!' She pointed at me, her voice rising. 'She called him names.'

'Names?' echoed Ben. 'What names?'

'Midget, Sir! And Snowflake. And Short-arse.'

'He did all this because she joked about his *height*?' His voice was incredulous.

'Yeah, and she said he had dandruff. He was really angry, Sir,' Molly continued defiantly.

Ben stared at her until she shifted uncomfortably in her seat. Eventually he spoke, waving the iPad in the air. 'I can't believe what I'm hearing. She called him a couple of names, so between the pair of you, you cooked up this hate campaign?' He pointed at Molly. 'You wait here.'

Turning to face me, he said under his breath, 'Why didn't you say anything about this?'

'I didn't know about it till now, I swear.'

Louder. 'OK, Lara. You go to Mrs Ellis's office and tell her everything, please. And I mean *everything*. This ends right here and the rest of you . . .'

He addressed the spellbound class. 'Get your books out and carry on reading from, erm, last lesson. Please.'

I followed him into the empty corridor as the room erupted behind us.

'Molly's boyfriend set fire to your *hair*?' he whispered.

I nodded then shrugged. 'Yeah, but only a bit.' I pulled the shrivelled strand down to show him.

'God, he could have scarred you for life. *Killed* you.' He shook his head slowly and stole his hand into mine. 'Why didn't you tell me it had got this bad? I could've stopped it.'

'I didn't want to get you involved,' I said. 'And I thought I could handle it on my own.'

'Right. Well, I'm going to make sure this is sorted out once and for all. You go to Mrs Ellis, like I said. I'm going to the boys' school to speak to the Head there. OK?'

I nodded. He kissed me quickly on the lips and smoothed down my hair then left, Molly's iPad still tucked under his arm. As I turned, I looked into the classroom through the little window in the door. And there was Chloe, her eyes almost popping out, mouth wide-open in a comic *Did I just see what I think I saw?* pose, which would've been hilarious under any other circumstances, but at that moment was so very much *not*. I knew straightaway: *She saw. She knows.*

I didn't know what else to do; I headed for Mrs Ellis's office.

'Lara, you should have come to me long before it

'reached this point,' she said, echoing Ben, when I finally finished telling her my tale of woe.

'But I couldn't before because of her blackmailing me about my mum's job. And I didn't know about the Facebook page until today.'

'Well, what I am going to do now is ask Molly to come and see me and hear her version of events. Then I shall ring both your mothers to –'

There was a knock at the door and her secretary came in, looking flustered.

'Could you come back in a minute, Mrs Davis, please?'

'It is rather urgent, Mrs Ellis,' she said, casting a glance at me.

'Lara, could you wait outside a moment, please?' I got up and stood in the corridor. They spoke in hushed tones, but I could still hear every word.

'What? *Our* Mr Jagger? Ben? Are you completely sure?'

'Yes,' Mrs Davis replied. 'I've just had the Deputy on the phone. Apparently, he told the secretary he had an important message, then punched the boy in the face. They believe his nose is broken.'

I almost fell on the floor.

'And where is Ben now?'

'According to Dawn, the secretary, he's already left the premises. I assume he's gone home. He hasn't returned to his class anyway.'

Mrs Ellis was silent for a moment. 'Thank you. I think Jean Muirhouse is free now. Could you find her and ask her to cover Ben's lesson and then send Lara back in, please?'

Somehow I found myself back in the office. 'Miss?'

'I'm afraid I have a serious matter to attend to, but I promise I will deal with this as soon as I can. In the meantime, can you please go back to lessons?'

She hesitated, an odd expression on her face, like some vague memory had begun to rise to the surface.

'Yes, Miss.' I said, leaving before she could work out Mr Jagger punches Sam Short + those reports of Mr Jagger and Lara alone = something's up.

But of course I didn't go back to class. Instead I raced out of the front door and into the car park, scanning the rows of vehicles for a knackered little silver car.

Nowhere.

Dug in my bag for my mobile, my hands trembling so much it took me three attempts to input the pin. It rang and rang and rang.

I cycled out of the gate at top speed, barely even registering the road as I ploughed into the flow of afternoon traffic.

My phone went before I'd gone half a mile. Pulling up abruptly on the pavement, I answered breathlessly without even glancing at the screen.

'*Ben?*'

'Lara? Is that you? I've just had Mrs Ellis's secretary on the phone. She said you're not in school.'

Not him.

'I'm . . . I'm on my way home, Mum,' I said, desperately blinking back hot tears.

'Are you all right? She told me there's been a problem and to come and see her, but I'm working now, then Gran's got her chiropody appointment at five.'

'It's nothing major,' I said. 'Honest.'

'OK,' she said. 'Tell me at home. I'd better go now anyway. You have remembered you're babysitting till I get back, haven't you?' Of course, after everything that had just happened, it'd gone straight out of my head. 'Don't forget to give Simon his tea. And ride carefully, please.'

As soon as she hung up, I tried Ben's number again, but it went straight to voicemail. As it did the time after that. And the time after that.

I stood at the side of the road with absolutely no idea what to do next. *Chloe. Mrs Ellis. What are they thinking right now?* And while the traffic roared past, my guts churned and I threw up, convulsively heaving until my stomach was empty. God knows how I made it home in one piece. I was shaking so much I could hardly see, never mind steer.

I *still* haven't heard anything so I can't sit here any longer, I'm out of my mind with worry. I've decided to leave Mum a note and take Simon with me; I'm going to Ben's house to make him tell me what's going on.

Later . . . My mobile rang while I was zipping up Simon's coat. I left him in the hall and took the stairs to my room two at a time.

'Where have you *been?*'

'Sorry, I was getting so many calls I couldn't deal with it; had to switch it off for a while to think.'

'Why on earth did you hit Sam?' I asked. 'I thought you were just going to report him.'

'I didn't plan to hit him, I swear. But when I told him I needed a word about what I'd seen on his girlfriend's iPad, he put such a cocky, arrogant smirk on his face that

I lost it. Totally lost it.' He half laughed. 'When I think of him setting light to your hair, I'm surprised I didn't kill him.'

'What happened then?'

'I don't know; I didn't hang about, to be honest. Did you speak to Mrs Ellis?'

'I told her everything, like you said. She's getting mine and Molly's mums in. When they know the truth, they'll see Sam got what was coming.'

He non-laughed again. 'I don't think that's going to matter much now for me. I've well and truly burnt my bridges at school. In fact, today marked the end of an extremely short teaching career. I haven't even started paying back my student loan yet.'

'But when they know what Sam was up to, they'll get why you did it, won't they?'

'I punched a student, Lara,' he said. 'Losing my job is pretty much a given. All I can hope for now is, once Sam's family know the circumstances, they'll be understanding and not press criminal charges.'

'The circumstances?' I repeated.

'Not you and me, God, no!' He sounded shocked. 'Lara, if that comes out, I have *completely* had it. I mean the Facebook page.'

My whole body went icy cold.

I chickened out telling him about Chloe. Or about the suspicion dawning on Mrs Ellis's face. Instead I swallowed hard and steeled myself to speak normally.

'You're about to leave anyway,' I said.

'Doesn't matter. I'm finished,' he said. 'I'll be barred from teaching.'

'I'm so sorry,' I said, and it sounded lame even to me.

'You don't have to be sorry,' he said. 'You've done nothing wrong AT ALL.' He paused then said, 'Lara, please promise me you won't say a word about us, no matter what questions you get asked. Not until we've come up with a story both of us can stick to. Once they start wondering why I hit Sam instead of dealing with it through the correct channels . . . well, we need to tread very carefully.'

'I'll be careful,' I answered.

He sighed. 'Look, sorry, but my head's all over the place. Can we talk later?'

'Of course.'

'OK, I'll ring in a bit.'

I said, 'I lov–' But he'd already hung up.

THEN, as soon as she came in through the door, Mum went, 'Lara, when we were getting Gran's bunions done, she said she's barely seen you for weeks. What's going on?'

The phone ringing cut me off before I could stammer a reply. Thank you thank you, Dad.

I immediately fled upstairs but I can't hide in my room forever. When Mum comes up, I'm going to pretend to be asleep. If she tries to talk, I'll say Gran's gone doolally, but I didn't want to say anything because she's already so stressed.

Shit!

What if she adds it to what Themnextdoor said about hanky-panky in the park?

OK, then I'll have to say I *have* been seeing someone, but it's some boy from school, and I'm sorry I lied before. That'll work: she'll be annoyed, but it'll be OK if I say I was too embarrassed or something.

OH MY GOD! Suppose she mentions it to Dad and he says something to Emma? She'll have to say what I told her about Ben in Cambridge.

Fuck. Fuuuuck. Fuck. I am *fucking* fucked.

Oh Jesus, the biggest shitstorm imaginable is about to strike. Mum, Dad, Gran, Emma, Chloe, Themnextdoor, Mrs Ellis . . . how long have I got before one of them works it out?

JUNE 16TH

It's only half four, but there's no point trying to sleep now when I've got to get up for the papers anyway. I've been texting him all night, but he hasn't answered once; I rang again about five minutes ago, but I couldn't even leave another message because his inbox is full.

Been crying so much there's nothing inside me apart from this hollow, sick ache. What am I going to do? Once they find out, they'll say we can't see each other ever again and I can't live without him. I wish I could work out who it's going to be so I could prepare, but it's impossible, like catching fog.

Finally, Ben's just rung! Said he's had his phone off because Dawn Grumpy Cow Secretary keeps ringing, but he's going to change his number today. He asked me delete all the text messages and voicemails from him 'just in case'.

Good idea. I will . . . later. I need to copy them down into here first. He's written such beautiful things, they deserve to be kept forever, not wiped away.

Later . . . Done the papers, come home. Told Mum I'm off round to Gran's for lunch and I am (briefly), before

I go to Ben's. Luckily, Simon's had another paddy over Dad missing his birthday so she's all caught up with him.

Not luckily, I don't mean 'luckily'. Poor Simon.

God, what kind of selfish cow am I turning into? Wish I could help, but I just can't think about anything else now, only trying to sort this mess out.

I've decided I won't tell Ben people are getting suspicious. He doesn't need that right now. We need to focus on sorting out the Sam stuff. I know we can get through this. As long as we love each other, we're invincible.

Loads later . . . I think I'm in shock. I should be howling, smashing up the furniture, but I feel calm. Kind of numb.

Turns out we're not invincible after all.

It's gone half ten and Mum's downstairs with a bottle of wine, watching the usual Saturday night rubbish on telly. Simon's been tucked up sound asleep for hours. Dad'll be watching the football highlights with Uncle Andy. No doubt Gran's in her chair in front of the TV too; maybe she'll have nodded off already. And I bet Molly, Mikaela and Chloe will be tarted up and out in town.

Me? I'm holed up in my bedroom, waiting for the knock at the door.

I thought I had it covered. I'd rehearsed all the possible outcomes in my head; every conceivable permutation of *who* and *when* and *where* and *how* the shit would hit. And then out of a blue sky, a curveball like a lightning bolt blew our secret open in the worst imaginable way.

I dropped in on Gran at lunchtime, then headed straight over to Ben's. Even trowelling on the make-up couldn't hide my red nose and puffy eyes. He took one look and pulled me into a massive hug as soon as I stepped in the hall.

'I've been dying to do that all day, I was dead worried you wouldn't come.'

He looked so gorgeous despite the bags under his eyes and his hair spiky from running his hands through it, the way he always does when he's stressed out. I put my arms round him and hugged him tight, loving the way he felt against me with his whole body telling me he'd keep me safe and things would be OK.

'Do you want a cup of tea?'

I shook my head. 'I'm all right for the minute, thanks. I just want to know what's happening.'

We sat down side by side on the sofa. He held both

my hands, lightly stroking them with his thumb while he filled in the missing parts of the story. As far as he could anyway.

'I've had a load of messages from school, Dawn too, but nothing else. I've been expecting the police round since last night, but no sign yet, so I don't know what's gone on with Sam, whether they're pressing charges or what. I've no idea what'll happen. Anyway, I've bought another sim card so don't ring my old number any more. You'll have to put this new one in your phone. Did you remember to delete the messages, like I asked?'

I nodded, *massive pants on fire* (I'll do it as soon as I've finished writing this). He got his mobile out to text me the number, sighing, 'I have had enough of everyone.'

Everyone? I couldn't help it, I burst into tears.

He looked dismayed. 'But not you. Oh, Lara, not you at all.'

'But it's all my fault! You must hate me. If it wasn't for me, none of this would've happened.'

'How is it your fault?' he said, holding me so close I could feel his heart beating through his shirt. 'Don't blame yourself. You're the victim here.'

He lifted up his hands and held my face. 'If it's anyone's fault it's mine for letting my temper get the better of me. Though no way do I regret punching that little bastard.' He leaned in and kissed me on the lips. 'How could you think I hate you? I love you more than anything.'

'But what about your career?'

'Screw my career, I'll get another one. I've got you and that's all I need.'

He kissed me again, but this time we kept on kissing. And kissing. And kissing. Then my hands were under his shirt and his were inside my top. When we finally broke apart, the atmosphere had changed and my entire body was burning.

'We don't have to do anything, you know,' he said, tucking his shirt back into the waistband of his jeans.

'I know,' I said. 'But I want to.'

We looked at each other. Then I stood up and held out my hand, and without another word we went up the stairs.

Afterwards, we lay in each other's arms and I was the happiest I've ever been. For the first time in my whole life, I had the feeling of being in absolutely the right place at the right time with absolutely the right person; of loving someone completely and being loved back in return; 100% certain that everything in my life had been leading to this man and this moment.

But maybe even then a bit of me knew it couldn't last.

The sound of traffic drifted through the open window and I knew I should be getting home, but I couldn't bring myself to leave. We'd been dozing, chatting and kissing for hours and I felt safe there in Ben's bedroom; like a princess in a tower with all the wickedness of the world shut out on the other side of the door.

And that's why, drowsy and contented, neither of us heard a single sound: not the key in the lock, not the front door opening, not the footsteps creeping along the hall then up the stairs. Nothing at all, in fact, until the bedroom door was flung wide open.

'I knew it!' shouted Dawn. 'I knew you were seeing someone else!'

We leapt apart and I dived completely under the covers while Ben pulled them up to his chest. I'd been visible only for a couple of seconds, but it was enough time for Dawn to register who was in bed with her ex.

'I know her!' she said. 'Oh my God, that's that student, that skinny ginger girl who went on your Cambridge trip. What's her name? Clara? Lara? Tit-something. The one Sam Short's supposed to have been bullying.'

I could hear Ben frantically scrabbling for his boxers

and felt the mattress buck beneath me as he jumped out of the bed, 'What do you think you're playing at?' he yelled. 'Get out!'

'What am *I* playing at?' she screeched in return. 'What are *you* playing at, you fucking paedophile!'

I peeped over the duvet and caught a glimpse of Ben's naked retreating back. Dawn was clomping down the stairs in front of him and they were making no effort to keep the noise down; I could hear every word as clearly as if they were still in the room.

'Get out of my house! And give me those keys NOW!'

'Have them!' I heard the jangle as she slammed them on the wooden floor, 'You dirty bastard. No wonder your phone was off. So that's why you hit that kid; you must be absolutely bricking it.' The front door was open now and I went to the window to see Dawn half walk, half stumble out on to the path like she'd been given a good shove from behind 'God, I thought you were in deep shit before, but this – shagging a schoolgirl. You *pervert*.'

As I looked down, she glanced up. I yanked the curtain across, but it was too late.

'You dirty little slut,' she yelled. 'You've had it too, when I ring the police.'

Ben shut the door and slammed both bolts across with such force the walls seemed to shake.

'Lara?' he called, running back up the stairs. 'Oh, love.'

I was trembling convulsively, from shock, I guess. He pulled me into his arms. 'Sssh, shhh, don't worry, it'll all be all right.'

But I think we both knew it wouldn't be. *Really* wouldn't be.

I had to go pretty soon after as Mum was expecting me home. Ben asked if I wanted him to come in and speak to her, but I said, 'What's the point?'

I mean, she'll find out soon enough.

Ever since then I've been waiting for the police to turn up. Waiting and waiting and waiting.

There's nothing I can do but wait.

JUNE 17TH

Dad came back from Little Dunmow last night. Neither him nor Mum have shouted at me once, even when it came out how much I'd lied. They're being all 'go easy on Lara' and 'have another hug' like I'm terminally ill or something. Bringing me toast and tomato soup, stroking my hair, speaking in v-e-r-y calm, v-e-r-y soothing tones.

Q. So why aren't they throwing furniture at me? Grounding me? Calling me all the slutty names under the sun?

A. Because, astonishingly, they think I've been *groomed*!

The police made this ridiculous deal of the iPod. 'Has he ever given you any presents? Or money?'

I told them about it, thinking they'd see it as evidence of how much we love each other. But no; apparently this is evidence he was *grooming* me.

They set me up, I am so *naïve*.

'I'm predicted ten A* GCSEs!' I shouted at the policewoman. 'I think I would know if I was being groomed.'

Is he at a police station? Is he in prison? Is he at home? Is he OK? I don't even know. No one will tell me anything. They keep saying not to worry about him and to focus on myself. I'm in a nightmare and I can't wake up.

Ben was right when he said they'd twist it, with their sick minds. The police must come across genuine cases of grooming all the time, like all that stuff that's in the news about paedophile rings and sex trafficking;

it's warped their way of seeing things. They're looking at us reflected in a fairground mirror, making up this distorted, sinister version of the truth.

'Hasn't your boyfriend ever bought you a present?' I asked the Family Liaison Officer, but she didn't reply.

Even Mum and Dad, who know me better than anyone, can't see the truth when it's slapping them across the face. They know I'm not some gullible, giddy featherbrain. *As if* I am going to be manipulated into doing anything I don't want to.

When I close my eyes, I see him lying next to me in bed. I can almost hear him breathing and feel his arms around me. Feel his skin. The pure, clean version of that afternoon, not their dirty, perverted account; that's what I'm clinging on to.

The Truth.

JUNE 18TH

They referred to me as 'the victim' all the way through my statement. I keep telling them, 'He's the victim, not me,' but nobody is listening. In the end I refused to say another word about it, just parroted, 'No comment, no comment,' like on TV.

I'm not allowed to see him or speak to him; I don't even know where he is. Even if I had his new number, Mum confiscated my phone this morning and banned me from using the internet unsupervised. I'm having to keep this diary physically on me at all times. One tiny good thing was I've always hidden it under the wardrobe, so when Mum searched my room (which I'm assuming she must've done), she missed it.

They won't let me leave the house, even to do the papers. What next? Food trays through a hatch in my bedroom door? Chemical toilet by my bed? Strip searches?

Later… Oh my God, oh my God! OH GOD!

My phone! Ben's messages . . .

I never deleted them!

JUNE 19TH

I climbed out of my bedroom window tonight. Scraped my leg to ribbons on the trellis, but managed to jump on to the flat roof over the garage before Dad came running out.

'What are you doing?' he said. 'You're going to kill yourself.' I made a dash for the gate, but he was too quick. Themnextdoor came out to gawp as Dad dragged me into the porch. ˌ

'Why won't you let me talk to Ben?' I screamed. Mum was white-faced and strained; she reached out to put her arm round me, to pull me into the hallway.

'Lara, love. Calm down, please.'

There's an unexpected freedom in having already smashed all the rules. Once there aren't any left to break, then you can do whatever you want and it doesn't matter.

I slapped Mum's cheek so hard my hand stung. Then yelling, 'Get off me!' I tried to run, but Dad blocked my way. Mum stepped behind to corner me and I was trapped.

Impulsively, I grabbed a picture off the wall: my school photo from Year 7. I hurled it at her feet and the frame splintered, sending shards of glass skittering across the hall. A piece flew up, catching Mum on the chin, and she brought her hand up. Blood trickled through her fingers while my eleven-year-old face smiled up at her from the floor.

Blood. Mum's shocked expression. Dad panting from exertion.

I slumped down, holding my head in my hands. 'I just want to see him,' I said. 'I just need to know he's OK.'

Mum and Dad both knelt down gingerly among the fragments of glass and put their arms round me.

'He hasn't done anthing wrong. We love each other.'

'I understand, love,' said Mum, kissing my head. 'It's all right. I understand.'

But she doesn't. No one does.

JUNE 21ST

The Family Liaison Officer came round again today. Jesus, I hate her guts, monstrous old hag. She's got a moustache which she obviously bleaches, but not very well because it's all gingery. Walrus Face.

I don't even know what the point of her is. She makes out she's listening, but she doesn't *hear*. Puts her 'professional caring' mask on: slightly furrowed brow? Check. Sympathetic nod? Check? Take no notice of what Lara is actually saying? CHECK.

Today she told us that because Ben has pleaded guilty there won't be a big trial so I won't have to give evidence. The text messages I forgot to delete were 'perfect proof'. And she delivered this bombshell in a smug, *Isn't that such great news?* voice, each heart-stopping word gift-wrapped and tied with a poisoned bow.

I left the messages there. He said to delete them and I didn't. I gave them their 'perfect proof'. Handed them Ben on a plate.

I couldn't take another word. I needed her to SHUT HER MOUTH. So I lunged at her, catching her off guard.

My mind and body have become two entirely separate entities. While my mind is hovering like a CCTV camera, unemotionally monitoring what's going on, my body is going mental and attacking a Family Liaison Officer.

I need them to see he is NOT guilty. He's being a hero, saying what they want to hear to protect me. Why? Because he loves me.

I WANT to give evidence, I tell them. I WANT to stand up there and explain how much we love each other. That we have done NOTHING wrong. But no one listens to me. Not Mum, not Dad, not the police and definitely not Fat Walrus Whiskers.

Ben hasn't made me a victim; they have.

JUNE 23RD

Mum and Dad informed me at teatime that we're all moving down to Little Dunmow 'until this business blows over'. Informed, not asked. Who I love, where I live . . . it appears I don't have a say in any aspect of my own life any more.

They haven't published my name in the papers, but everyone round here knows. I'll be the *girl who had an affair with her teacher* forever. The police and the press have hijacked me and Ben and warped what we had, turning it into something dirty and wrong. And that's where the gossips get their opinions from. I'm the only one telling the truth, but no one listens.

'I'm not going,' I said, staring at the table, deliberately ignoring the new lines etched on Mum's face. And the two stitches in her chin.

'Lara . . .' said Dad, his voice sounding a warning.

'It's OK, Tony,' said Mum quickly. 'Remember.'

A recent conversation flashed between them in that one word. *Remember . . . Lara's been sexually exploited? Lara's a mental case? Lara's ruining our lives?* I left and went up to my room, passing Simon, wide-eyed and silent on the landing.

I understand all the 'fresh start' blah blah blah.

But if we move away, how will Ben know where to find me?

JUNE 26TH

His solicitor forwarded a letter from him.

It had an official stamp to show it had been 'cleared' for me to see. A personal letter addressed to me; a private letter that was crumpled and covered in other people's fingermarks before it even reached my hands. Mum and Dad have read it, the solicitors have read it, the courts have read it, the police have read it and the last person to get to read it is ME.

All these strangers debating whether or not it's in my 'best interests' to see a letter from my *boyfriend*. Deciding whether it will help me get 'closure'.

What a fucking joke. The last thing on earth I want is 'closure'.

Sam posting topless pictures of me on the internet was hell enough. But now that the authorities have stripped me naked to gawp at and comment on, I understand what it's like to be *truly* humiliated. The most intimate details of my life have been shared with strangers. Sam did it because he's a bully; the authorities did it to 'protect' me. Can't they see? Their motives might be different, but the outcome is exactly the same.

They've put our relationship under a microscope. We've been dissected and studied like a body on a slab and now dozens of people have had their grubby minds and their grubby fingerprints all over my letter before I even knew he'd written it.

Dear Lara,

I am so sorry for what you're going through and for my part in it. I never meant to cause so much pain to so many people, but especially to you. I know you'll be angry that I've pleaded guilty, but please believe me when I say I am doing it for you. I've already brought you too much grief to put you through a trial.

What I'm trying to say is I want you to forget about me, to move on with your life and be happy. None of this is your fault, please don't blame yourself for anything. You have done nothing wrong. I was selfish and stupid and my biggest regret is the impact my actions will have on you.

Ben

Forget about me?

Move on?

Nothing wrong?

I've done nothing wrong. WE'VE done nothing wrong. Why would he say that to me? 'Selfish' and 'stupid' for showing me what love means?

I keep rereading it, looking for coded messages hidden in the first letters of every noun, or every third word, like Enigma. I've tried so many possible combinations, but I can't find what he really means. Wherever the key is to unlock the truth, I can't find it.

The only other explanation is that someone forced him to write this garbage: his solicitor, or Walrus Woman, or the police. Ben could never write something like 'move on with your life'.

He must realise that, without him, I don't *have* a life.

JUNE 30TH

I want to see him. I want to run up, throw my arms round his neck and kiss him until we both gasp for air. I want to lie in his arms in the afternoon, sleepy and content just to be with him. I want him to show me off to his family and friends. I want him to teach me to drive. I want him to talk to me about films we're going to watch together; books we're going to read; countries we're going to visit.

I want to hear him say, 'I love you.'

July

JULY 2ND

I didn't bother getting out of bed today. Mum came up three times to leave food outside the door, but I'm not hungry. I can't imagine feeling hungry again.

I wish I could just go to sleep and not wake up.

JULY 4TH

I'm looking at the world through a pane of glass. I can't touch anyone and no one can touch me. I've used up a lifetime's worth of feelings and now I'm empty.

They'll never let me see him again.

JULY 7TH

Mum got the doctor round today. I think they're worried I'm going to 'do something I'll regret'.

I told them I've been doing things I regret since birth, but if it's a euphemism for pulling my own plug then no worries, I won't be going there. *Lara Titless Deserves to Die* was Sam and Molly's antisocial media campaign, not mine. I wouldn't give them the satisfaction.

JULY 10TH

Over three weeks since I last saw him and I know I'll never see him again.

There's no point to anything any more.

Move on, he says.

Someone tell me *how*.

JULY 11TH

Just had an email from Emma. She keeps ringing but she seems to have finally got the message that I am never speaking to her again, the TRAITOR.

Anyway . . . words of wisdom from my dearest cousin.

Lara,

I know you're angry with me, but I didn't have any choice. I couldn't lie to the police, could I? And anyway, even though you might hate me now, I'm hoping if you understand where I'm coming from, you might forgive me and be mates again.

I know you and I know you really, properly loved him. And I know he wasn't some textbook paedo who stalked you and jumped on you. Or a power-mad perv who set out deliberately to find a teenage girl and use her for kicks. And I totally believe Ben is an entirely different person from the one who was written about in the papers, and that he genuinely loved you.

BUT that doesn't make what he did OK. I had to tell the police what I knew because Ben had committed a crime against you. It didn't matter what his motives were or whatever his feelings were, he should <u>NEVER</u> have acted on them because –

DELETE email

That's as far as I got. I don't know why she even bothered. The evil snitch.

DELETE Emma

JULY 14TH

Moving day.

We're about to set off for Little Dunmow. There was a time when I would've been thrilled by this, but since Emma turned supergrass it's the last place I want to be. Mum and Dad have signed the rental on a house near Uncle Andy's. Haven't packed much, just a suitcase, but I've got a feeling we won't be coming back. Not for a while anyway. The furniture's going into storage.

Me, Mum, Dad, Simon – we're on the move for the third time in three years.

No access to the internet – they've still got my phone and my laptop, even my iPod. But they never found this diary. I have become devious.

Can't risk it being discovered in Little Dunmow either, so it's making a final journey to the storage unit. Safer this way, hidden in the bottom of a holdall with my old teddies.

Without Ben, what do I have worth writing about anyway?

I know I won't see him again.

They're waiting outside. I can hear Dad slam the boot on the last of the stuff. Simon's chasing Paddington round the garden, giddy, the pair of them.

All my memories of Ben are in these pages. From the first time we met, when he was just a teacher. The show, Cambridge, the kiss and our one afternoon together. Four weeks, that's all we had together, that's all, but my whole life changed, I changed. He has taught me to be proud of who and what I am. For the first time I can remember, I am happy being me. Inside me, I carry it like a light: Ben thought I was worth losing everything for. And I guess that's why I don't need to keep reading about him over and over. He's a part of me now.

Mum's shouting up the stairs. Time to go.

AFTERWARDS

Ben,

Sometimes, out of the corner of my eye, I catch a glimpse of a guy with scruffy surfer hair and a show-stopper smile and I spin round, heart racing, expecting to see you. But it never is.

My counsellor told me that this happens to everyone who has suffered an 'emotional bereavement'. It was her idea to write this letter as 'catharsis'. Because I never got the chance to answer your letter during the trial, she reckoned doing it now might give me a sense of 'closure'. She said we can send it to your solicitors and maybe they'll forward it on. If it's 'appropriate'. (When she talks, I hear inverted commas 'around' 'nearly' 'every' 'word'.) Actually, being mean there. Talking to her has really helped me to come out of the past year as a fairly sane person.

You know, it's been over a year since I last saw you

and the same since I last went to school. I had a kind of meltdown and stopped eating and went to stay in a clinic for a while. But I'm back to normal now, more or less. My GCSE results were OK, by the way. Not the full house of top grades, but a decent sprinkling. Surprising how well I did, considering. And, guess what? One of the A*s was English literature. I'm sure you'll be pleased to hear that.

You're out of prison now; they told me that much. Maybe you've gone to the States or Australia or somewhere so far away to put me behind you and make a fresh start.

And speaking of that, I've had a fresh start of my own. We upped sticks and went to live in Little Dunmow, near Emma. I'm starting Year 12 at her college in a few weeks and I get to see her all the time, which is just excellent. And I've picked English lit as one of my A levels: I think that'd make you happy too.

Did you change your name? I looked for you on the internet, but I only get old news stories about you and me. Maybe you're not allowed. Or maybe you don't want to be found. We changed our name to Merry. After all the gossip, it seemed the best way and, ironically, dealing with the fallout of you and me brought Mum and

Dad closer, and now we're all under the same roof again. Even when I was being awful (you can't imagine what a nightmare I've been), they were incredible. Simon's settled in OK at his new school and Gran's living in a sheltered housing place nearby. Dad's working. Money's not so tight.

Life is good.

Did they tell you what happened to Molly and Sam? Both excluded from school, plus Sam got dropped from the football team. Serves them both right. Molly's parents were mortified and so nice to Mum when they found out, so all that stress was for nothing. I'll never make that mistake again. Me and Chloe are on friendlier terms nowadays and she's still seeing Rob, who cut Sam dead when he found out what had gone on. Seems like a decent guy. She sent me this five-miles-long email full of heartfelt apologies and how ashamed she feels. She wants to come and visit soon. We'll see.

OK, next: my BIG BOMBSHELL

I've got a boyfriend.

He's called Joe, he's seventeen, he plays the drums, he likes reading, he makes me laugh and he makes me feel good about myself. You taught me how important that is. He's one of the crowd that Emma hangs about with in college. I really, really like him, but I'm not sure if I love him. Maybe love isn't always instant.

And I suppose the L-word brings me to the point of this letter: *YOU*. If this letter is going to be an exercise in 'catharsis' and 'closure', I need to write about you.

Wow, this is *hard*. (You can't tell, obviously, but about ten minutes of pen-chewing and wall-staring have gone on between these two sentences.)

How do I feel about you now? Here goes . . .

When my world was a sorry tangle of school horror and rows at home, you came along and blew it all away. When I thought you loved me, I felt like a goddess. None of the other troubles touched me any more because I had you, and having you outweighed any misery. When I saw myself through your eyes, I knew what I was worth and that gave me the confidence to stand up, to feel proud of who I am, to fight back. And to not give a flying fuck what anyone else thinks.

That hasn't gone away.

At the trial, the prosecution said you 'groomed' me. Everyone kept saying I was the victim, but it didn't feel that way. Victim of the police and the law maybe. But you? No way. Then, when you got sentenced, I fell apart. Not only because I knew I'd never see you again, or I'd smashed up the lives of my whole family, but because I thought it was my fault for not deleting those text messages. Mum, Dad, Simon, Gran, Emma – all those lies I told. And you most of all, sent to prison, your career over before it even started because of me. Thinking I'd dragged you into something that had destroyed your life.

There were days when all I could do was stay in bed and stare at the ceiling, *totally hating* myself. I was so confused. What I saw as love, they said was exploitation. You weren't my boyfriend, you were a criminal. On and on until the ground started shifting under me and I couldn't stay upright. I couldn't concentrate, or sleep or eat. Getting your letter, I think that was the hardest thing to cope with. I felt utterly abandoned.

That's when I got ill.

So that led to three months in a clinic having 'therapy' (so American-sounding). And the biggest lesson that taught me was that none of this is black and white. Every single person affected by what we did sees it from a different angle.

So here's my perspective: I absolutely worshipped you. There's no way I could have stopped that any more than I could grow wings and fly to the moon; even if you'd completely ignored me forever. You and I both know you tried. You backed off after that night in the car when Mrs Ellis told you to steer clear.

Do I think you groomed me? No I don't. I think you felt sorry for me. You knew I was head over heels in love and you wanted to show me that I wasn't all those things Sam and Molly made me out to be; that I was special and beautiful and worth something. Probably flattered too; who doesn't want to be adored? And you were lonely: new job, new town. And then of course there was Molly offering herself up on a plate. If you were just some sleaze, you'd have gone for her, not me.

And this is the conflict at the heart of everything. I loved you, you loved me and we both chose to ignore the GIANT carved-in-stone fact you were my *teacher*. How stupid were we to think that love was bigger than that?

My parents told me they sent me to school as your pupil, not your girlfriend. I told *them* I was afraid and alone; every aspect of my life was a struggle, then you came along and taught me how to make it better. I *know* you loved me, Ben, and nothing you ever did made me feel forced or uncomfortable.

BUT

I have been over this in my head so many times. Seriously, if thoughts were legs, I'd be a gazillionipede. But now I understand: just because something feels right doesn't mean it *is* right.

I had a blazing crush on you that must have been so obvious from when you pulled up at the bus stop to save me from Molly. You said it too, that night in the pub in Cambridge, remember? Some cosmic force sent you to help me. And you had the power to give me that help . . . as a TEACHER, but you fanned the flames of my crush until everything caught fire. You should have walked away before we fell in love. You were the adult, it was your responsibility to put the brakes on, not kiss me that night in Cambridge. If you'd walked then, I'd have just been a girl with a crush on her teacher and you'd still have the job you loved.

I built our relationship up into some kind of Romeo and Juliet fantasy, us against the world. And because we loved each other, breaking the rules was OK. You know, the rules are for ordinary people, but not for us; we're special kind of thing.

Not true.

All the counselling has made me understand that the teacher/student boundary exists for a reason and crossing it is never right. It's a big wall as high as a mountain and it is in a place where there IS such a thing as black and white. I had nearly a year of total hell before it finally clicked: even when something feels right, it can still be wrong.

So how do I feel a year on? Life's good in Little Dunmow. I've got good friends and me and Emma are closer than ever, and my family is back in one piece again. And Joe may or may not be The One, but I like him enough to hang around while I find out. Maybe that's exactly what I need: to fall in love with someone else to finally find my 'closure'. And if I can't say I love Joe today, well, tomorrow – who knows? Maybe one day in the not-miles-off future, when I see a guy with scruffy surfer hair, my heart won't skip a beat in that split second before he turns around.

Wherever you are, whatever you're doing and whoever you're with, I want you to know, I'm doing OK.

And I hope you are too.

Love, Lara xx

ACKNOWLEDGEMENTS

First, a massive thank you to my agent, Anne Clark, and my editor at Egmont, Stella Paskins, for all their support, advice and commitment to *Me & Mr J*. I feel incredibly privileged to be working with both of you. Swiftly followed by immeasurable thanks to Emma Swift, Rebecca Fewster and especially Amanda Pawliszyn, for your invaluable advice and honesty with the early drafts. Without your enthusiasm, I would have given up. And ditto Ross MacIntyre, Christina Kiley and Edward Kiley.

All the characters sprang from my imagination, but I have borrowed some names for the nice characters. If you share a name with one of the less pleasant ones, it is totally coincidental, I promise.

Lara and Mr J's story is also entirely fictional and teacher/student relationships are newsworthy precisely because the overwhelming majority of teachers are dedicated professionals who would never abuse the trust placed in them. I have been fortunate enough in my working life to meet many fantastic teachers whose commitment to improving the lives of young people is inspiring. In particular, I'd like to mention the incredible staff and students at HNC, especially those in the English department. Cheers for all your patience and encouragement.

But above all, I would like to say thank you to Tim Bolton. Without your kindness, belief and love, I could never have written this book. I am so grateful.